Return to Love
Betsy St. Amant

Published by Steeple Hill Books™

STEEPLE HILL BOOKS

**Steeple
Hill®**

Recycling programs
for this product may
not exist in your area.

ISBN-13: 978-0-373-87540-5

RETURN TO LOVE

Copyright © 2009 by Betsy St. Amant

All rights reserved. Except for use in any review, the reproduction
or utilization of this work in whole or in part in any form by any
electronic, mechanical or other means, now known or hereafter
invented, including xerography, photocopying and recording, or in
any information storage or retrieval system, is forbidden without
the written permission of the editorial office, Steeple Hill Books,
233 Broadway, New York, NY 10279 U.S.A.

This is a work of fiction. Names, characters, places and incidents are
either the product of the author's imagination or are used fictitiously, and
any resemblance to actual persons, living or dead, business establishments,
events or locales is entirely coincidental.

This edition published by arrangement with Steeple Hill Books.

® and TM are trademarks of Steeple Hill Books, used under license.
Trademarks indicated with ® are registered in the United States Patent
and Trademark Office, the Canadian Trade Marks Office and in other
countries.

www.SteepleHill.com

Printed in U.S.A.

If you, O Lord, kept a record of sins, who could stand? But with you there is forgiveness; therefore you are feared.

—*Psalms* 130:3–4

To my daughter, Audrey. You were with me from the beginning of this novel, even before either of us knew. I love writing books with you!

Acknowledgments

Thank you to my husband, Brandon—
your encouragement keeps me going. I love you!
Also to my parents—deadlines are much easier to
meet when you willingly babysit! And to my
Super Agent, Tamela, and my awesome editor
Emily—you guys are the best.

An extra special thank-you to Tom Dyer at the
Aquarium of the Americas. You answered endless
questions about your beloved birds, and I'm so
grateful for your patience and help.

And a huge thank-you to Dallas Weeks, a talented
singer, songwriter and friend who generously allowed
me to use the lyrics to "Blue Eyes" in this story.

Chapter One

Feeding time—Gracie Broussard's favorite part of the day at the Aquarium of the Americas. It was worth the chaos, watching a dozen or more awe-stricken young faces press against the display glass in glee. Sometimes she didn't know who bounced the most—the excited children, or the penguins.

She stroked the top of Ernie's slick head, then leaned over to check the thermometer in the pond. Still sixty degrees. She wiped her wet fingers on her khakis. Ernie let out a high-pitched squawk.

"I know, little man. I feel the same." She grinned and adjusted the microphone clipped to the collar of her tan polo. Time to perform. Several families were already gathered in the dim walkway. One child mashed his lips against the glass and made a fish face.

Gracie smiled. She used to be nervous speaking in front of the visitors each day, but the more she did it, the more she realized the facts and statistics she rattled off during the short presentation were all but ignored in light of the spunky black-and-white birds at her feet.

"Hello, there, and welcome to Aquarium of the Americas. I'm Gracie, and these are my favorite guys in the world." She gestured to the penguins, some perched on the rock display, others diving into the murky waters.

Her assistant Jillian entered the exhibit through the side door, a five-gallon bucket of fish in her hand. The penguins waddled toward her on cue. Huey and Gumbo fought for position on the slippery rocks, and a little girl in the hallway laughed.

Gracie brushed some feathers from a boulder near the pond and perched on the edge as Jillian settled beside her, notebook balanced on her knees. "These are African penguins, and as you can tell, they're just a *little* hungry."

The adults smiled and the children pressed their hands against the window as if hoping to reach right through and touch the birds.

"As I tell you about my friends here, Jillian will record the data of each penguin's feeding habits. These records help us determine which penguins are sick, and which species of fish each bird prefers."

Gracie plucked a slimy squid from the bucket at her feet and offered it to Ernie. He mashed it in his beak once, then tossed up his head in approval. The fish slid down his throat, with a little help from his tight neck muscles. Jillian jotted the note in her record book.

"Most of you probably know penguins can't fly." Gracie tossed a fish to Gumbo and glanced at the group gathered around the glass as she reached for another. As she continued to expand on the many wonders of her feathered friends, she let her gaze wander over the gathered crowd. She stopped mid-sentence when she saw a familiar mop of curly brown hair and a pair of broad shoulders.

Her heartbeat quickened. That hair, that stance... No, it couldn't be, not here in New Orleans. She'd left him—no, actually, he'd left *her*—seven years ago on his parents' private dock on Cypress Black Bayou Lake. Walked away with that guitar pick he was always fiddling with, a curt nod of his head...and her heart. But regardless how much time had passed, there was no mistaking the dimple in his chin or that square jaw.

Gracie's heart pounded in her chest, and she was sure the

crowd could hear it on the other side of the glass. *No, no, it can't be him.* But the truth refused to be denied.

The sleeves of his rust-colored sweater were pushed up to his elbows, revealing the muscular lines of his forearms. She couldn't help staring through a foggy lens of memory. Those strong, tanned arms that once hoisted her from the murky waters of the Black Bayou onto the pier, that wrapped around her shoulders in comforting side-hugs, that arm-wrestled her for a week's worth of chewing gum, now were crossed firmly over his chest—a much wider, broader chest. Laugh lines softened the once hard planes of his face, and a layer of dark stubble clung to his lower jaw. Time had been awfully fair to Carter—which was a lot more than he deserved.

Anger choked in Gracie's throat and a headache sprang to life behind her eyes. She stumbled over the rest of her speech. "Penguins can't fly because their bones are solid, n-not hollow like other birds."

Did he recognize her? It had been so long…and in some ways, not nearly long enough. Her traitorous gaze darted in his direction again, and their eyes met. His thick eyebrows rose in slight acknowledgment, and her stomach gave a telltale leap.

Her emotions might not remember Carter's betrayal, but her heart did. It remembered every labored, bruised beat.

After seven years, Carter Morgan Alexander was back.

Carter Alexander stared into the penguin exhibit, reeling from shock. He had no idea when he dropped his suitcases at his friend Andy's apartment and headed to the aquarium for an afternoon of sightseeing that he'd run into *her.* When had Gracie left Benton, LA, and moved South? It'd been, what— about seven years now?

Mouth dry, he struggled to keep a poker face as Gracie's piercing blue-green gaze settled on his. It was full of questions, accusations—and more than a little anger.

Something unfamiliar and tight stirred in his stomach, and he leaned against the wall, arms crossed. Good thing, since his knees were starting to feel less than sturdy.

Gracie finally lowered those arresting eyes, and a slight blush crept up her neck and into her cheeks as she reached forward with a fish. She looked the same—the elegance that always clung to her persona like a robe of righteousness still seemed to fit. And that long red hair…she hadn't cut it. It cascaded over her shoulders like a flaming liquid waterfall.

Much like it had the night he broke both their hearts.

Carter briefly squeezed his eyes shut against the memory and tried to focus on the penguins darting about the tank. Gracie might not have changed much since that starry summer night on the lake, but he sure had experienced a transformation. The problem was, judging by the stiffness in those slim shoulders, she wasn't planning on giving him a chance to prove it. He should have tried years ago—then again, fresh anger wasn't any easier to handle than stale.

Carter shifted his weight against the wall. He deserved her ire. Let Gracie remember him the way he was—the arrogant jerk with a guitar and a dozen girlfriends, the lead singer of the band Cajun Friday who was too big for his britches, his faith…and his best friend.

Gracie's musical voice sounded over the speakers, just as soft and clear as the regret that haunted his mind these last several years. "It's a common misconception that all penguins require an arctic atmosphere. Many people are shocked that we have such a large exhibit here in this sultry part of the South—and it might surprise you that we keep the air in this tank regulated to seventy degrees."

She stroked the back of one of the birds, who seemed determined to creep closer to the bucket of fish. Jillian nudged the barrel out of reach with her foot.

Gracie's eyes found Carter's and then flitted away. "I've learned that everything isn't always what you might expect."

She finished her presentation, but it was nothing more than a blur of statistics and red hair gleaming under the aquarium lights. Carter's throat tightened and he applauded with the rest of the crowd. The penguins preened, as if they knew they were the real stars of the show.

"Are there any questions Jillian or I can answer?" Gracie tucked a lock of hair behind her ear and smiled, though her eyebrow quivered in the way it always used to when she had a headache.

"What's that penguin's name?" One blond kid raised his hand and then pointed to the bird standing alone at the edge of the water.

"This is Garth." Gracie moved toward the penguin and he brayed up at her. "Sorry, Garth, the fish are all gone."

The kids giggled. An elderly man in suspenders hooked his thumbs through the straps and called out, "Any baby penguins around right now?"

Gracie shook her head. "No, but we're hopefully bringing in a new colony soon, and we have high hopes for eggs then."

Carter felt his hand rise of its own accord. Gracie's eyes landed on him and she sucked in a sharp breath, audible through the speaker system. "Yes, you in the back?"

Demoted to a curt *you*. He lowered his hand. "How long have you worked here?"

Gracie smoothed the front of her polo shirt over her pants. "A little over two years. Anyone else?"

A kid started to shout a question but Carter interrupted, louder. "Where did you get your education to work with the penguins?" Might as well find as many answers as he could, while she was forced to talk with him. Because afterward…

"A marine biology degree from Nicholls State University. In Thibodaux." Gracie's brows met in a pained arch. "Next?"

"Do penguins respond to music?" Carter's muscles relaxed as Gracie's seemed to tighten. That was the girl he knew, the one who bunched under pressure but held her own with a grace that still knocked his breath away. He fought the grin on his lips.

"Sometimes we play the radio for them. They seem to enjoy it but prefer speaking to each other instead." Gracie licked her lips and turned toward the other side of the crowd, effectively dismissing him. "I'm afraid that's all the questions we have time for today. Thanks for coming, and enjoy the rest of your visit."

He'd pushed too far.

The families slowly began to disperse, but Carter remained fixed against the wall, his legs unable to move and his heart unwilling to let them. He had to see her, talk to her again. But what would he say? Sorry for the last seven years of silence? Sorry for that night on the pier that ruined a lifetime of friendship? Nothing seemed sufficient, nothing seemed capable of quelling that distrust in her eyes or the rigid body language that all but screamed *get away from me*.

She'd never believe the truth even if he told her.

And why would she? Disloyalty was all she knew from him, all he'd ever bothered to show. Regret coated his stomach and Carter blinked against the emotion rising in his throat. Seeing Gracie after all this time rendered him somewhat senseless. He was a changed man now—though it was maybe a little too late to do any good.

Gracie strode out of the aquarium, shoving her hair back with both hands and closing her eyes briefly before disappearing from sight. Yep, she had a headache. He knew it as surely as he knew her favorite color was blue and her favorite song was "Over the Rainbow." She hurt because of him—and not for the first time.

Hindsight offered startling new clarity. If he hadn't been such a fool, things could have been so different. Carter rubbed his forehead with his fingers, trying to hold back the torrent of memories demanding release. Not now, not here. He'd wait until he was back with his old college buddy Andy, maybe sprawled in front of the TV with a Dr. Pepper and some popcorn before he'd vent. Maybe Andy would have more words of wisdom to share, some advice to remind him he wasn't the bad guy anymore.

Then maybe that look in Gracie's eyes would stop tormenting his heart.

Gracie braced her elbows on the glass display case at the front of the gift shop and buried her face in her hands, drawing in a slow, deep breath. The aquarium was closed, yet

Carter's presence continued to throb like a sore wound. How dare he show up after so long and invade her workplace? His father had contributed large donations to the aquarium for nearly a decade, yet Carter picked *today* to pop in? He could have found out where she was years ago if he hadn't turned his back on his family, as well as her. The last few years of his silence had been punishment enough—she didn't need this jolt of surprise now.

She raised her head and looked across the counter at Lori Perkins, her best friend and manager of the gift shop. "I need more coffee."

"Here." Lori shoved a foam cup across the counter. "I just got a cappuccino before I locked up. You need it more than me."

"Thanks." Gracie propped on one elbow and took a sip of the warm liquid. Much better—though her head still ached behind her right eye.

"I can't believe I missed seeing him." Lori swung her long brown hair over her shoulder and hunched down to mimic Gracie's pose on the counter. "Is he as cute as he was on his last CD cover?" She winked.

"That's not the point." Gracie grabbed a pencil from the display beside the cash register and twirled it through her fingers. Anything to avoid eye contact and Lori's I-dare-you-to-try-and-keep-a-secret-from-me gaze. They'd shared coffee and more than their share of confidences over the past year as roommates, but this was different.

This was a broken fragment of her heart.

Lori plucked the pencil from Gracie's grasp and stuck it back in the case. "Okay, so we know he's probably still a looker. The awful ones usually are."

"There was something different about him." She squinted, trying to recall the specifics of the memory. "Something in his eyes."

"Maybe he's sorry for the past and came to apologize." Lori grabbed a dust cloth from under the counter. "Sometimes regret changes a man, rare as it might be." She grinned and went to work cleaning the inside of the glass.

Gracie stepped away from the counter to give her room. "But he couldn't have known I was here. We haven't talked in seven years."

"He couldn't have contacted your mother? I thought you said your families were close once upon a time." Lori sprayed cleaner over the top of the case and rubbed. "I'm sure there were ways if he was determined."

"What if he's here for something else, something that has nothing to do with me at all?"

"Isn't that what you want?" Lori set the bottle on the counter and tilted her head to one side. "To be left alone?"

No. Yes. Gracie shrugged. "I guess so."

"Girl, you've got it bad, even after all this time." Lori shook her head and resumed her cleaning.

A familiar ache started in the base of Gracie's stomach until it filled her insides with a heavy layer of regret. "Even if I do, it doesn't matter." She looked away, the ache doubling in intensity. "It never did before."

"What do you mean?" Lori paused, holding the rag inches above the countertop.

"Carter was my fairy tale, never my reality." Gracie picked up a stuffed penguin dressed in a tuxedo and squeezed. "He was just this dream I had until I grew up." She snorted. Dream, misunderstanding, mistake—same difference.

"So what happened?"

Gracie set the penguin down and sadly adjusted its little black bow tie. "I realized some toads never turn into princes."

Chapter Two

Carter flopped down on the sofa and propped booted feet on the coffee table. His friend and college roommate, Andy Stewart, handed him a Dr. Pepper before claiming the La-Z-Boy. "Here you go."

"Thanks." Carter opened the can and took a quick sip, the fizz bubbling in his throat on the way down.

"So what's up, man? You that nervous about performing for the kids?" Andy jacked the handle on the recliner, and the footrest popped into place.

"Not really. Your youth group at *L'Eglise de Grace* can't be worse than the crowds I've played before." Carter shook his head with a grin. "And if they are, we have a whole new problem on our hands, Pastor."

Andy laughed. "Hey, I've done what I can with them. But they're still teenagers—so no promises."

"Hopefully they won't throw rotten vegetables."

Dr. Pepper spewed from Andy's lips. He sat up straight and wiped his chin with his hand. "People have actually done that?"

"Well, not veggies. But a drunk guy threw a shoe once."

"No wonder you retired."

Retired, quit. Was it the same? Not really, but Andy knew the details, knew that Carter's faith was what led him to leave the stage lights and his band far behind. If not for his friend's guidance, he would have put down his guitar permanently, but Andy convinced him to try singing in churches instead of in clubs.

Nothing had been quite the same since.

"If you aren't nervous about performing Thursday night at my church, then what gives? And don't pull the jet-lag card on me—you only drove about five hours to get here."

"I ran into someone today I wasn't expecting." Carter took another gulp from his soda can. "It didn't go so well." To put it mildly. He waited at the aquarium for Gracie until closing time, when he was politely asked to leave by a security guard who needed to lock up. Gracie had successfully avoided him after the penguin's showing—not that he really blamed her.

"Must have been a woman." Andy's eyes darkened with understanding as he leaned forward to rest his drink on the coffee table. "Ex-girlfriend?"

"Sort of." He and Gracie had never dated, thanks to him. But if he could go back...

Carter couldn't sit anymore, not with the weight of the past pressing against his shoulders. He stood and moved to the window in the living room, shoving aside the curtain to look down onto the road below. A streetcar stopped at the corner and passengers filed out—a tall brunette in a long, camel-colored jacket, a potbellied man in overalls, a teen boy with spiked hair and a studded dog collar. The rest of the patrons followed behind, adjusting their jackets and purses, some talking, others holding hands. A few walked with their heads down, arms crossed, as if the city or maybe the world itself were out to get them.

He recognized that stance. Carter rested his shoulder against the wall, eyes fixed on the fading golden sunlight spilling over the streets. He knew how it felt to hide, to grow tired of the mask. He walked around with his own arms crossed in a protective gesture for most of his life—the result of a fishbowl existence, lost within the murky waters of his father's church. People thought they saw everything, but they only saw what they wanted. Never the truth.

The streetcar moved away from the corner and continued down the block, out of his line of vision. He let the curtain fall and turned back to Andy.

His friend studied him with narrowed eyes. "I'm not sure if I should offer to pray with you or give you the remote control."

Carter snorted and sat back on the couch. "Now I know you pity me. You never shared the remote in college."

"You were hardly there, anyway." Andy's eyebrow quirked. "Day or night."

"Don't remind me," Carter groaned. "The life of a rockstar." His guitar, propped in the corner of the room near the fireplace hearth, caught his eye and he winced at the memories. How many screaming fans and busted strings and bright lights had it seen? Too many to count—though those days were all but over. Church crowds didn't react quite the same way to his music.

"Sacrifices are never simple." Andy nodded. "You had a big one to make."

"Funny thing is I don't miss it."

"Not even a little?"

Carter shrugged. "Maybe a little." He'd been lead singer of Cajun Friday for years. He never would have thought a high school band could have lasted so long and gained so much popularity in college and beyond. But if he was serious about honoring God with his life, he was more than willing to start from scratch and do things right this time, do something big and meaningful with his future as his parents always hoped he might—even if his dad wasn't around to see it happen now. Bitterness clogged his throat and he coughed.

"I can't wait to hear you play again." Andy edged the recliner back a notch and stretched out. "Those kids wear me out, but they're pretty awesome. Some of them have come in off the street with the hardest hearts you can imagine, and done complete one-eighties."

"I'll bet." The description sounded like Carter himself not too many years ago. "I hope I'm able to reach them."

"I'm sure you will. Don't sweat it." Andy pointed toward the ceiling. "That's His job, right?"

"Right."

Silence stretched across the room, save for the ticking of the coffee mug shaped clock on the living room wall. Could Andy tell he was still thinking about Gracie? Carter shifted on the couch, not sure whether to bring up the past on his first evening in New Orleans or let it ride for now. He pressed his lips together.

Andy made the decision for him. "Okay, I'll take one guess and then leave you alone. Is this about Blue Eyes?"

Carter's breath caught. His nickname for Gracie in high school, after that wide, naively alluring gaze—not practiced, as most of the women who kept him company—and the inspiration behind one of his band's hit songs. If she wanted nothing to do with Carter now, that was her choice, and an understandable one—a few years ago, he would have felt the same. But the swells of pride and stubbornness had washed him away from what his heart knew to be right, tugging him further out to the sea of bitterness and denial. How could he have been so blind to what was right before his face for literally a decade? But he'd ridden that circular method of thinking for years now, with no more clarity than before.

He needed to answer Andy's question, though he was sure by then his friend could read the truth on his face. "Yes."

"Then here you go, man." Andy tossed the remote at Carter from across the room. "That's all you had to say."

On Wednesday morning, Gracie poised her pencil over the paper in front of her, wrote a figure, then erased it. She grimaced. It was no use. Regardless of what she scribbled in the margins, the money simply wasn't there. The gala budget was already stretched to the max, and she had yet to fund the decorations.

You have to spend money to make money. The words of her boss, curator of birds Michael Dupree, echoed in her mind from last week's meeting. That might be true, but she couldn't create something from nothing.

Gracie kneaded her forehead with her knuckles. The framed picture on her desk of Ernie and Huey caught her eye and she grinned in spite of her circumstances. They were waddling toward the camera, chests puffed out and beaks open as if smiling. "Guys, remind me why I volunteered to head this fund-raiser again?"

But the photo was evidence enough in itself. She was doing this for the penguins upstate who wouldn't have a home come March. The Louisiana Aquarium, after struggling to recover financially from the results of Hurricane Katrina, would be shutting its doors in the spring. Because the other aquariums in the state were at full capacity, the Aquarium of the Americas was the only possible solution for the little birds that would soon be homeless.

If she could raise the money. The board of advisors firmly stated they were willing to expand the current exhibit if the funds were provided. It wasn't in the yearly budget otherwise—not after their own financial hit from the storms.

Gracie tapped her pencil on the sheet before her. She would have to call in some favors unless she could move money from another category. But most of what she needed had already been purchased, or required a set amount she couldn't budge. For instance, the caterer and the band. If she was better at begging, she might play up the charity angle and attempt to get a price cut from either—but at the moment, she simply didn't have that much moxie.

She sighed. Two weeks ago, before the budget was finalized, she felt prepared, capable and ready to take it all on. Then she started receiving quotes from the seemingly endless list of vendors necessary to pull off the gala, and her hopes dwindled almost as fast as the cash in the temporary account.

"I've got to make this work." The penguins in the picture didn't respond.

Gracie rolled back in her chair and closed her eyes. Not only was the destiny of a group of innocent birds counting on her, but in a way, she felt pressure even from beyond the grave. Carter's father—Reverend Alexander—was the one who had secured her job at the aquarium. The penguin exhibit had been one of his favorite places in America—hence his generous annual donations. She had fought to have this new wing named in his honor. If she failed the penguins now, she failed Carter's father—the one man in her life who'd been a constant. He deserved better than that, especially after the way Carter had treated him. She *had* to figure something out.

The office door opened and Lori flopped into the chair across from Gracie's desk. She tossed her a rubber penguin keychain. "Here, we got a new shipment. From the blue cloud gathering outside your office, I thought you might need cheering up."

"Am I that obvious?" Gracie squeezed the belly of the penguin. A light shone from its open beak and she laughed.

Lori crossed her legs. "So it's not going so great, huh?"

"It *was* going great until I realized our money ran out and we still need decoration funding, not to mention extra advertising dollars." Gracie rested her elbows on the desk. "What kind of Christmas gala is it going to be if no one hears about it, and there's all this great food and entertainment in a completely bare, boring room? We want to wow the people so that they'll donate money to fund the new exhibit."

"What if I did it?"

"Did what?"

"Decorate! You know I went to design school for a few years. I majored in creating on a low budget." Lori winked.

"Did you minor in creating on no budget?"

"Hey, in college—same difference."

Gracie squinted, trying to envision the possibilities. Maybe her friend was on to something.

"My stepmother loves this aquarium. I bet she'd donate a bunch of poinsettias for the cause, and I can go to the dollar store and load up on lights and ornaments for a tree." Lori's eyes sparkled with excitement. "And you know those wreaths in our attic I usually hang on the windows at Christmas? I can let you use them for the gala instead."

"That might actually work." Hope sprung for the first time in hours.

Lori tossed back her long hair and tilted her nose toward the ceiling. "Of course. I'm a genius."

Gracie's cell phone rang next to a stack of papers on the desk. She flipped the cover, still smiling at her friend's generosity, and said hello.

"Ms. Broussard?"

"This is she." Gracie didn't recognize the voice. She picked up a pencil and grabbed a pad of sticky notes in case it was fund-raiser-related.

"This is John Stevens with the Creole Boys band."

"Yes?" A knot stuck in Gracie's throat, but she tried to think positively. John could be calling to confirm the dates or—

"I'm afraid I have some bad news about your event."

Gracie clenched the pencil with suddenly sweaty fingers. "Oh?"

"The Creole Boys are going to have to cancel."

Gracie rubbed her bare arms against the cool fall breeze blowing off the river. Late autumn had officially arrived in all its glory, scattering golden leaves across her path and casting dusky shadows under storefront awnings.

After Lori finished her closing duties at the gift store, they decided to share a bowl of gumbo at Gumbo Shop before heading to their townhouse. They could brainstorm what to do about the gala over a steaming bowl of sausage and rice. Her mouth watered just thinking about it.

Lori tugged down the long sleeves of her uniform shirt. "Whew! It's getting chilly."

"You'll warm up after a few bites." The hanging wooden sign of the famous restaurant swung into view. Gracie quickened her pace and breathed in the spicy aroma hovering outside the door. A few more steps, and she'd be inhaling the best gumbo this side of the Mississippi. She reached for the handle, her stomach growling in anticipation.

A deep, familiar laugh penetrated the air.

Grace's fingers slipped off the door and she stared unseeing down the street. The bustling city sidewalks, the resonance of wind and boots scuffling leaves faded until only one sound reached her ears. Her back straightened and she drew in a deep, shaky breath. "Did you hear that?"

"What? Your stomach growl?" Lori reached for the door of the restaurant.

"No." Gracie shoved the door shut and pulled Lori to one side. "That laugh."

Lori frowned. "I hear people laughing all the time. It's a common expression of pleasure or enjoyment. You should try it more—"

"It's Carter." Gracie slumped against the wall by the door. The husky, unique chuckle sounded again from the corner, and she knew without looking he must be a part of the crowd gathered around the performing street mime. His voice wrapped around her soul, pressing forbidden memories into the cracked pieces yet to heal. She'd missed that laugh.

Lori's eyes widened. "Are you sure?"

Oh, she was sure. Her heart knew his voice—the same voice that serenaded the ripples in the Black Bayou Lake, that sang reassurances when they were ten years old and snuck out to watch a meteor shower and got lost on the way home. The same laugh that echoed across the dirty lake water while splashing waves in her face. No, she wouldn't forget it— couldn't. She nodded once.

"Let's go talk to him."

"Are you crazy?" Gracie stared at Lori in shock. "I don't want to talk to him." Yet some morbid, curious piece of her did.

"He's famous around this area, Gracie. You've gotta admit that's pretty cool, jerk or not." Lori craned her head to peer up the street at the patrons gathered around the clown.

Bitterness crept back into the hollow places and Gracie's fists clenched at her sides. It was always about Carter and his music, never about anything else. Never about his family— the way he hurt them with his rebellion and didn't care. The way he broke his poor father's heart by leaving town and never looking back. Never about his schoolwork and responsibilities, never about getting good grades for college, never about the church and the youth group.

Never about her.

His laugh sounded again, rising above the other chuckles in the crowd, and it sounded closer this time. Panic pounded in equal rhythm with her pulse. She couldn't sit inside the Gumbo Shop now, couldn't spoon rice from a bowl knowing Carter was mere feet away.

"Let's just say a quick hello." Lori tugged at Gracie's arm. "I want to see the man who's had you all stirred up for a decade."

"Seven years."

"Whatever." Lori pulled, and Gracie's feet reacted against her will, following her friend down the cracked sidewalk and up the street to the corner of Royal and Saint Peter—her traitorous heart only an anxious beat behind.

Carter joined in the crowd applauding the mime's antics, then reached for his wallet and dropped a dollar bill into the box at the clown's feet. "Great show!"

The mime bowed in his direction and pretended to swipe tears of appreciation from his painted cheeks.

Andy laughed. "See, I told you this was better than reruns on TV." He elbowed Carter's arm.

"I never doubted you, man."

"I really like supporting the entertainment around here. We haven't had nearly as many acts since Hurricane Katrina."

"I would imagine not." Carter moved aside for another couple to drop a handful of change into the box, briefly wondering how much money the mime made on an average day performing. Was he a flood victim? Surely this wasn't his only job.

It reminded Carter he had a lot to be thankful for—the money he'd saved from his touring days and album releases guaranteed financial security for the next several years, if he was smart. Then he could work a side job and live comfortably while figuring out which path he was to take with his music ministry—while attempting to right the myriad wrongs in his life.

And better yet, not having to touch the inheritance money his father left behind. He didn't want any money from his father—ever.

Ignoring the tightening in his stomach, Carter turned away from the crowd. "So what's this about New Orleans cuisine? Are you guys all talk down here?"

Andy puffed out his chest. "Hey, we don't joke about food in this city. You want some jambalaya? The Gumbo Shop is just around the bend."

"Lead the way. My stomach will follow."

Carter moved behind Andy, and a flash of red on the corner caught his eye, hovering under the elaborate ironwork balcony on Royal Street. He blinked, then stared. It was Gracie, standing beside a tall brunette, both of them leaning against the window of an antique gallery and looking right at him.

Gracie ducked behind Lori and turned to face the La-Branche House, heart pounding as she pretended to study the lacy iron scrollwork dripping off the three stories above her head. "Did he see me?"

"Probably. Just go talk to him, for old times' sake. You know you want to introduce me."

Oh, right. Gracie allowed Lori to pull her across the corner. *Trusted new best friend, meet my backstabbing old best friend.* They drew closer and Gracie's pulse leaped at the sight of Carter's unruly curls falling across his forehead. It brought another rush of forgotten memories and she paused, nearly yanking Lori backward. "You know, I'd really rather prefer a big bowl of gumbo. I'll even pay." She tried to tug her arm out of Lori's grasp but her friend squeezed tighter.

"No, ma'am. We're almost there. Then you'll thank me for getting you past this nightmare."

More like forcing her through it. Gracie took a shuddering breath and crossed the remaining feet of concrete separating her from her past. A light breeze wafted her hair across her eyes and she tossed her head to free the strands, not wanting to see Carter up close but unable to quell the urge—or Lori's purposeful march.

Carter looked up as they neared. "Gracie." Warmth filled his eyes and a nervous shiver inched down her spine. "Hey. Wow, you look great."

So did he, but that was beyond the point. She crossed her arms over her chest and nodded, her back rigid. "Hi."

They stared at each other.

A man walking ahead of Carter stopped and turned around. Gracie gasped. "Andy?" The street suddenly seemed much, much too small. "You know Carter?"

"Pastor Andy!" Lori beamed. "Small world, huh?"

"Carter and I were roommates at LSU." Andy shoved his hands in his pockets and looked from Carter to Gracie, a knowing grin lighting his features. "And I guess you're Blue—"

Carter stepped forward, bumping Andy with his shoulder. He stretched out his hand toward Lori. "Carter Alexander."

"Lori Perkins, Gracie's roommate and friend from work." They shook hands.

"Well, isn't this cozy." Andy smiled. "We were just about to grab some gumbo. You ladies want to join us?"

"Sure." Lori beamed.

"No, thanks," Gracie said at the same time.

Gracie exchanged looks with Lori, hoping her friend would catch the hint in her glare, but she instead turned to Carter with an innocent, wide-eyed expression. "So I hear you visited the aquarium yesterday."

Gracie sucked in her breath. Now Carter would know she had been talking about him. She tucked her hair behind her ears and risked a glance at his reaction.

Surprise crossed his face, followed by…amusement? He nodded once, his shoulders relaxing. "I did."

"Did you enjoy it?"

Gracie wished it wouldn't be immature to kick Lori in the shin.

"Yes, actually." Carter's eyes left Lori's and collided with Gracie's. "Beautiful sights."

Andy snorted, then coughed loudly into his fist.

The heat in Gracie's face morphed into an inferno, and she wished the sidewalk would swallow her whole—her flaming cheeks, blotchy neck and shaky hands in one big gulp.

Lori pulled in her bottom lip, but a smile poked around the edges of her mouth. "I'm glad you thought so."

Andy gestured toward Lori and Gracie. "These ladies here have been volunteers with our youth group for over a year now. They've been a big help."

"I'm sure." Carter smiled, but it didn't reach his eyes. His mind was on something else—Gracie remembered that zoned-out look he'd get before starting a conversation he wished he didn't have to have. She searched for a way out, a way to back-pedal into a new topic. Her mind went blank. *Breathe, Gracie. It's almost over.* She'd somehow survive this encounter-that-should-never-have-been and record the entire brutal ordeal in her journal.

Then promptly burn the pages.

Carter cleared his throat, emotion dimming his eyes. "Gracie, it's been so long, I really—"

"Like we said, we were just heading to dinner." Gracie quickly gestured over her shoulder. She was being rude, but she couldn't bear to listen to whatever he had been about to say. Her heart fluttered faster than the humming birds outside her mom's old garden. "So I guess we'll see you at church to-morrow night, Andy."

"Sounds great. Carter will be there, too, playing for the youth."

Lori's mouth opened. "I didn't realize you were this month's entertainment! I can't wait to hear you play."

"Thanks." Carter smiled, but his disappointed gaze stayed on Gracie's, searching, seeking—what? Acceptance? Forgiveness?

She flexed sweaty palms at her sides. "It was nice, uh… nice seeing you."

"You, too—and nice meeting you, Lori. I hope to visit the aquarium again." He edged back a step.

"How long are you in town?" Lori squinted up at Carter against the fading evening sun.

He shrugged. "Not sure. Why do you ask?"

"Gracie is hosting a fund-raising event at the end of next month. A big Christmas gala, to raise money for a penguin expansion project at the aquarium." Lori shook off the hand Gracie laid on her arm. "You should come. It's for a great cause."

Gracie's cheeks continued to burn. What was Lori up to? The fund-raiser was none of Carter's business. Irritation settled in her stomach, replacing her Cajun-food craving.

"Like I said, I'm not sure how long I'll be here." He glanced at Gracie, then back at Lori. A slight grin tipped the corners of his mouth. "But I imagine 'bout as long as it takes."

"Perfect." Lori tossed back her long hair. "Then you should still be here for the dedication. It'd be great for you to cut the ribbon in honor of your father."

"My father?" The smile faded from Carter's face and his eyes darted to Gracie in alarm.

Her heart skipped, then thudded hard against her chest. This wasn't exactly the way she had planned on telling Carter about the new wing being named after the reverend. In fact, she hadn't planned on telling him at all. He wasn't even supposed to be here. Did he have to ruin *everything* that was important to her?

Lori glanced back and forth between Gracie and Carter's narrowed eyes as if following a tennis match. "I hope that wasn't a surprise."

Carter shook his head, but the light remained extinguished from his expression. "It's not a problem." The frown between his brows suggested otherwise.

Gracie tugged on Lori's sleeve. "We better go eat before all the tables are gone." The restaurant wouldn't be booming on a weeknight, but she couldn't look at Carter a second longer.

Lori followed Gracie's pull and stumbled after her down the street. "See you guys later!"

Gracie tightened her grip on Lori's shirt and forced a smile at the men standing in their wake.

Not if she could help it.

Chapter Three

"Have you lost your mind?" Gracie's voice grated with frustration as she pulled her chair away from the table. The legs scratched against the concrete floor of the Gumbo Shop and she plopped into the seat with a glare. Carter and Andy had been seated on the other side of the outdoor patio—at least they'd taken her not-so-subtle hint about preferring to eat separately. Though after Carter's reaction to the new wing honoring his dad, she was a little surprised he hadn't turned and fled the city. Abandonment was his middle name, after all.

Lori raised her eyebrows in feigned innocence as she settled across the table and reached for her menu. "What do you mean?"

"You know exactly what I mean." Gracie snatched the menu from her friend's hands and leaned forward, her voice lowering to a hiss. "Are you trying to kill me with embarrassment? There's got to be a better way to go."

"Don't be silly." Lori took her menu again and opened it. "I'm just helping along the natural course of true love."

"True love?" Gracie nearly choked on the words. She rested back in the chair and crossed her arms over her thumping heart. "Maybe a decade ago, Lori. Not now. No way."

"I thought you said it was only seven years." Lori grinned. "Hey, want to split the crawfish étouffée?"

Gracie shrugged. Annoyed as she was, she had to admit the crawfish sounded pretty good. Her stomach growled on cue. "Fine. Whatever."

"You still buying?"

Gracie's throat clenched.

"Just kidding! I know better than that." Lori laughed. "Maybe I should get dessert to make it up to you. Chocolate brownie pie?"

Gracie chewed on her lower lip. Forgiveness would come at a price, all right—but what better payment than chocolate? "Okay, fine. *With* ice cream."

Their truce settled, the girls tucked the menus away and gave drink requests to the waitress.

"So what was that all about?" Lori leaned forward, resting her elbows on the table.

"What was what all about?"

"Carter's reaction to the new wing's name. He looked like he'd seen a ghost."

Gracie snorted. He probably had, in his mind anyway. No better way to heap shame on a man than by confronting him with one of his biggest mistakes. Served him right. "He was probably ashamed."

"I thought he left you, not his father." Lori frowned.

Gracie shrugged and averted her eyes, tired of the painful memories. "He left all of us."

The waitress arrived with their drinks, and Gracie gratefully stabbed her straw into the ice, glad for the distraction. But Lori wouldn't let it go.

"Do you think Carter will actually come to the fundraiser?"

"Not if I don't officially invite him."

Lori's gaze jerked to meet Gracie's. "What do you mean? You have to!"

"No, I don't. He wouldn't want to come anyway. If he did, it'd just be out of pity or some twisted form of obligation." Besides, she didn't want the extra headache of Carter's presence while trying to carry off the important evening. It was bad enough trying to choke down dinner knowing he was two hundred feet away. A lot was riding on the event's success, and she wouldn't—couldn't—let an unsettling blast from her past rob the penguins of their new home.

That is, if she didn't single-handedly determine their fate first by holding a gala with no band. She groaned inwardly.

"Well, you still have plenty of time to decide." Lori set her jaw in that stubborn way of hers.

Gracie crossed her arms, mimicking Lori's position. Fine, let her friend hope. It wouldn't do any good, but at least it'd keep the peace for the next few days. Lori would figure it out eventually—when it came to Carter, *no* meant *no*. Gracie refused to acknowledge another option.

She was finished putting her hope in him.

"Just so you know, 'It's a Small World' is playing in my head right now." Andy grinned at Carter across the table at the Gumbo Shop. "Who would have thought the woman you're so torn up about is none other than our Gracie Broussard?"

Carter glanced over his shoulder, even though he knew there was no way the women could hear them across the noisy restaurant. After Gracie's obvious lack of interest in eating together, he and Andy gave the girls a head start and requested a table on the other side of the patio. Now the aroma of fresh garlic bread and Cajun cuisine tickled his nostrils, but the weight of seeing Gracie up close did permanent damage to his appetite. He set his fork in his nearly full bowl. "It is pretty weird that she goes to your church. Talk about a coincidence."

"Maybe it's more than that." Andy sipped from his water glass, then squeezed another slice of lemon over the top. "I wouldn't assume if I were you."

"Point taken." He pushed his bowl away.

"Too spicy?"

"Just not hungry."

"Since when did a woman take away your appetite?"

Carter shrugged with a smile. "Since I grew a conscience."

"Even guilty people need to eat." Andy scooped a spoonful of rice onto his spoon.

"With all my regrets, if that wasn't true I'd be a stick." Man, he should have searched Gracie out over the past years. But what would he say? The proper apology or explanation still failed him. There just weren't words adequate enough to express his stupidity, his immaturity—sure, he'd been a high school kid at the time, but no one deserved the treatment he'd given Gracie and his family. No one deserved the prank he played or the things he said that night on the pier—the last time they'd spoken before today. Even if there were reasons behind it that she still didn't know.

Carter stirred his water glass with his straw. He thought he'd been protecting Gracie when he left. Hindsight, unfortunately, proved that hasty decision had backfired—and pounded the final nail in the coffin of their future.

"Everyone messes up."

"But not everyone stabs their best friend in the back." Just one of the many sins on his list. He'd had his chance with Gracie, and ruined it. There might never be full recovery from such a blow, but maybe he could stir up enough of their friendship to remind her of the good times, the times he didn't make her cry—if she'd let him.

"Gracie's got a good heart." Andy wadded his straw wrapper. "I'd give her the benefit of the doubt before you write off any chance of fixing things between you."

"Maybe you're right." Carter stared into the dark rue of his dinner, memories teasing the ripples in the broth. They'd been a good team, once upon a time. For instance, Gracie loved Oreos, but hated the cream filling. So they'd sit on the tall barstools at the counter in his mom's kitchen and he'd eat the filling while she dunked the plain cookies in milk. Then there were the days spent riding tubes on the lake, camping with his family, and fishing off the pier. They rarely fought as kids, but when they did, Gracie would win from the sheer logic of her arguments. Carter learned early on that keeping up wasn't worth the effort.

But her stubbornness could go both ways. Gracie was the only girl he knew who didn't mind baiting her own hook—she'd even beaten him in a youth fishing tournament in sixth grade. The girl could accomplish anything she made up her mind to do, including shutting him out now.

"Did you know she was planning on naming the exhibit after my father?"

"No, she never mentioned that part, but then she didn't know I knew you. There's no use dwelling on the past, man. You're a different person now." Andy slurped the last of the gumbo from his spoon and leaned back from the table. "You know that, right?"

"Most days I believe it." Carter started to look over his shoulder again but forced himself to face forward. No more looking back, wasn't that what Andy was trying to tell him?

"But not today?"

Carter shook his head.

Andy sighed. "I'll get you a carryout box."

"You know, it doesn't matter at this point if Carter comes to the gala or not. There won't be much of one without any entertainment." Gracie forced herself to pick her feet up from the floor instead of shuffle. She was trying hard not to have an Eeyore moment—as her mom always used to say when she started a pity party—but it was hard.

"Don't worry, Gracie. Something will work out." Lori shifted her Bible to her other hand and looped her free arm around Gracie's shoulders. "I still think your idea of asking Andy to get the youth group involved was a great one."

"Guess we'll find out in a little while." Gracie walked with Lori through the church office corridor toward the kitchen in the gymnasium. She needed caffeine—no, she needed *money*—and maybe a massage for the tense muscles in her neck and shoulders. So far she had a low advertising budget, a nonexistent decorating budget and no band. She hated to ask what else could go wrong, but really—what else could go wrong?

Lori dropped her Bible and notebook on the counter in the empty gymnasium and turned on the overhead lights. "The kids should be here any minute. You want a root beer? Or Diet Coke?" She moved toward the fridge.

"Diet Coke." Gracie sank into one of the folding chairs near the counter and laid her Bible on top of Lori's. She stared at the creased cover. God had always come through for her before—this time shouldn't be any different. Still, an urgency pressed on her heart. Or maybe it was dread.

Lori shut the fridge door with her hip and slid Gracie's soda across the counter to her. "Think positively. It shouldn't be too hard to find another band."

"A band for what?" Tawny Sinclair, a fellow youth group volunteer, breezed into the gym and headed for the refrigerator, her long brown hair streaming down her back in loose waves. "Any Diet Cokes left?"

"Two." Lori rested her elbows on the counter in front of Gracie. "We were talking about the situation Gracie mentioned during Bible study earlier tonight."

"Oh, yeah, the penguin thing?" Tawny flipped her bangs out of her eyes and brought her drink to the counter. "What about it, again?"

Gracie couldn't help but notice Tawny's low-cut sweater and hip-hugger jeans, not exactly church attire. Gracie sipped from her Diet Coke and studied the girl over the rim of the can, trying not to judge. Tawny had shown up for Bible study, and that was what really mattered. The rest would come in time.

Though apparently she hadn't listened all that hard to what was said during group prayer.

"Yes, the penguin thing. Gracie needs a musician for her gala, ASAP." Lori turned up her root beer, then wiped her mouth with her hand. "Not to mention some cash for the rest of the budget."

"It'll work out." Tawny flicked her fingers in the air, dismissing the topic. "So anyway, did you see that new shoe store that opened on the riverfront? Totally adorable."

Lori's face lit. "I did, but haven't been inside yet. Are they expensive?"

"Not for me." Tawny opened her drink can with the aid of one manicured red fingernail and smirked.

Lori narrowed her eyes.

"Tawny, what did you think of the women's class tonight?" Gracie interrupted before whatever thoughts Lori processed could escape. She sent her friend a *be nice* look. Tawny was still new to the singles group at the church—she seemed to honestly not realize how she came across to others at times, which was another reason why Gracie tried to befriend the girl. Everyone else seemed content to just gossip about her wardrobe choices and flirty behavior.

"It was okay, I guess." She wrinkled her nose.

"I'm glad you came. It's good to see you getting involved, I know that's never easy in a new church."

"Right. Thanks." Tawny tucked her leopard print purse out of sight under the row of cabinets. "I guess we better get the snacks set out for the youth, huh?"

"They'd find them even if we hid them." Lori washed her hands at the sink, then pulled a bulk package of cream-filled cookies from under the counter and began lining them on a tray. "They're like junk-food magnets. Or vacuum cleaners."

Gracie set out the paper cups and two-liters of various sodas. "I saw you helping them *clean up* last week." She snorted. "If they were vacuums, you were an industrial-strength machine."

"Whatever." Lori tossed a broken cookie at Gracie, who caught it just as the gymnasium doors opened with a bang. Several of the youth hustled inside, laughing and shoving each other. Andy followed close behind, Carter on his heels toting a black guitar case.

The cookie slipped from Gracie's fingers and crumbled on the counter. With all her worries about the gala budget, she'd forgotten about Carter's performance tonight. But there was no putting it out of her mind anymore—there he was, dressed in worn jeans with shredded knees and a black button-down shirt. His usually rumpled, curly hair was gelled, and he'd shaved yesterday's dark stubble from his cheeks.

"Breathe," Lori mumbled, nudging Gracie with her hip as she stowed the cookie bag in the cabinet. She waved and smiled at Andy and Carter, who were moving toward the makeshift stage set up near the front of the gym.

Gracie straightened her shoulders and turned away from the men. "Where are the napkins?" She could do this. She'd just stay busy in the kitchen during Carter's performance, then focus her attention after the show on the youth and on talking to Andy about fund-raising. No problem.

"Right here." Tawny spun around from ripping open a bag of chips and handed over the pile of napkins.

Gracie took them from her outstretched hand, then realized Tawny's gaze had locked on something over her shoulder. She turned to see Carter pulling his guitar from his case and strumming his pick over the strings. The soft melody echoed across the gym, carrying with it a sudden wave of memories.

Tawny's breath caught and a slow, cat-like grin eased over her features. "Who's the new guy?"

Chapter Four

Carter wiped a damp palm down the leg of his favorite jeans and reached to adjust his guitar strap. He just fixed it minutes ago, and it hadn't so much as inched along his shoulder, but he had to do something with his hands while Andy introduced him.

He risked a peek at the rows of teenagers sitting in folding chairs, arranged in front of the makeshift stage composed of wooden boards and a few screws. The amp and speakers were wired up, thanks to the church's tech guy, and they lined the edges of the gymnasium's platform exactly as he requested for optimal sound.

Gracie hadn't joined the crowd on the floor. She was avoiding him, it was evident in her tense shoulders and averted eyes—and the way she kept rearranging what looked to be a perfectly suitable display of snacks. Lori and another brunette had taken seats toward the middle of the rows of teenagers, probably prepared to do crowd control if they grew rowdy. An empty seat remained on Lori's right. Would Gracie join them later? Carter could only hope.

He flipped his favorite guitar pick between his fingers as he waited for Andy to finish making announcements, but before he could stop it, his traitorous gaze flitted back to Gracie. She was wiping crumbs off the counter into her hand.

Crumbs? They hadn't even eaten yet. *Come on, Gracie, give me a chance here.* His heartbeat quickened and he sent a quick prayer heavenward for strength. He had to show Gracie who he'd become—or she'd never forgive him.

Andy's voice booming across the gym jerked Carter back to reality.

"So be sure to look for the Six Flags sign-up sheet on the bulletin board in the office. And now, a man who really needs no further introduction, Mr. Carter Alexander!" Andy turned toward Carter and began to applaud. A few of the teens, mostly girls, jumped to their feet and clapped wildly.

Carter forced a smile to his face and thoughts of Gracie from his mind as he clamored up the stage and adjusted the stand to his level. "Hey, guys." His voice echoed louder than he meant and he eased off the microphone an inch. "How are we doing tonight?"

A few of the kids yelled back, some jumping up and down, others standing. A few boys in the back sat with arms crossed and scowls tattooed across their faces. *Tough crowd.* Carter fought another round of nerves. So what if not everyone here loved him? He wasn't here for his own fame anymore—thankfully, those days were long over.

"Play 'Lucky Lady'!" A guy with dreads on the front row called above the din. He grinned around a lip piercing.

Carter strummed his pick over the guitar strings. "Lucky Lady" was one of Cajun Friday's first big hits—unfortunately, the lyrics weren't exactly appropriate for a church crowd. "Sorry, no can do. What about 'Peace To You'?" Another Cajun Friday hit, but one Carter had tweaked after the band's break-up to offer new inspirational meaning.

The crowd cheered. Carter felt his muscles relax as he began the first bars of the familiar tune.

When the night is long and the music fades,
When all hope is gone when I walk away,
I wish peace to you…peace to you…

A few of the girls in the middle of the audience began to sway, arms around each other's shoulders. A lighter flicked on toward the back of the crowd, and Andy quickly moved to retrieve it, whispering in the boy's ear before pocketing the evidence with a stern expression.

Carter fought a grin as he continued to sing. Soon the sensation of being back on stage enveloped him with its familiar, welcome presence, and the nervousness fled away. He loosened up after the first verse, rocking out the chorus.

Peace to you, when nothing else is true.
Peace to you, when your world is black and blue.
I wish peace to you, the kind I know by heart...
Can we ever just go back to start?

The lyrics thumped a sudden, painful reminder of Gracie. *The music, think of the music—not the lyrics.* His fingers slipped on the strings, and he struggled to regain his place.

The teenagers began to sing, picking up the chorus with him toward the end, and they remained standing even after the last note was played. He eased into a familiar worship chorus next, then as the last note filtered through the room, he motioned for them to have a seat.

"Listen, guys, I know some of you are probably wondering why I'm not playing the songs I used to play. I'm sure you realize I'm not a member of Cajun Friday anymore."

A kid in the back booed, and Carter held up one hand. "I'd like to tell you why."

The teenagers quieted down, shifting positions in their chairs. Some leaned forward, slight creases between their brows. The nerves bounced back with a vengeance, and Carter swallowed hard. It was one thing to play on stage for hundreds of screaming fans, another to talk to the impressionable youth about their lives. His hands grew clammy, and a hundred doubts flooded his mind. Was he cut out for this? Would they listen to anything he had to say?

At that moment, a slight figure slipped from the kitchen

into the dim lighting around the rows of chairs and took the vacant seat between Lori and a young blonde.

Relief rushed through Carter's stomach in a warm wave and he instantly felt stronger.

Gracie had come.

Gracie fought the shockwave of memory assaulting her senses at the sight of Carter beneath a row of stage lights, guitar in hand, and microphone close to his mouth. How many times had she seen him in that very environment and sat in the front row, praying God would open his eyes to his feelings for her? Carter had to know how she felt all those years, had to know the secret she'd hidden long before she found the guts to confess.

Why had she even come? She'd told herself she'd stay in the back and remain focused on the kids. But something drew her to the chairs, almost against her will. Besides, she ran out of things to rearrange in the kitchen and Andy had started shooting her curious looks.

"You okay?" Lori whispered from her left.

Haley, a high school freshman with long blond braids, leaned forward from Gracie's other side and shushed them both. Her eyes were wide and she pointed toward the stage, as if shocked they would dare talk in the middle of such a performance.

"Sorry," Lori whispered. Her eyes locked on Gracie's and she raised her eyebrows, silently repeating her question.

I'm fine, Gracie mouthed. Lori's eyes narrowed, but she shifted back in her chair, apparently content to let it go for now.

Gracie faced forward and kept her eyes focused on Carter's guitar—not his face. She really should pay attention in case any of the teens wanted to talk after the concert. She wouldn't be much of a role model if they asked questions and she had to admit she hadn't been listening.

"The decision to quit the band didn't come easily. I fought what I felt I was supposed to do for weeks. But one night on stage, staring out into the foggy sea of smoking, drinking fans, I just froze. I couldn't make myself play." Carter grinned and rubbed his hand over his head. "It's like all those prayers my mama prayed finally caught up to me."

The kids snickered and Andy let out a hearty amen from the side of the gymnasium.

"I realized my musical career had become the most important thing in my life, and, well, God doesn't appreciate idols." He released a slow breath. "I took a gift the Lord gave me and twisted it into something that dishonored Him." The crowd hushed and Carter shook his head, staring down at the guitar draped across his torso.

A lump stuck in Gracie's throat and tears welled in her eyes. She crossed one leg over the other, and the squeak of her chair drew her away from the intensity of the moment. She stared at the stage lights, determined not to cry. Not over him—not again.

"I'm here tonight to encourage you not to make the same mistakes—and not just in music, but with any talent you've been given." A shock of curly dark hair fell over Carter's forehead and he shook it back with one quick motion, just as he used to do as a teenager. "Don't abuse the gifts. It's not worth it."

Gracie gritted her teeth at the irony all but slapping her across the face. To Carter, music always equaled a freedom of expression and rebellion. Yet now he stood on stage, telling kids not to do the same? It was the same concept of any "been there, done that" testimony, but still hard to swallow.

The inspiration that touched her soul moments ago faded into regret and she ducked her head as Carter led the group in a prayer. She pressed her fingers to her eyes, fighting back tears of betrayal and denial—betrayal of what Carter had done to their friendship, and denial of the emotions still churning beneath the choppy surface of her anger.

The prayer ended without Gracie hearing a word, and she stood woodenly with the others as Carter closed with a rendition of a popular praise song. Andy took the microphone when he was through and thanked him for coming, then announced that snacks and sodas would be handed out in the back of the gym.

The teenagers cheered and jockeyed to be first in line at the counter by the back doors. Gracie followed, hoping Carter wouldn't see her. She couldn't talk to him, not with annoying tears still clinging to her eyelashes. She made a beeline for Lori.

"Gracie, wait up!" Carter's unmistakable voice echoed across the gymnasium floor and she slowed her clipped stride. There was no denying she heard him, the entire gym probably had. She drew a deep breath and turned, fists clenched, ready to fake it until she could pour a few cups of soda and get out of there.

"I'm so glad you were here." Carter was out of breath as he jogged the remaining steps to Gracie's side. He grinned, that lopsided smile that used to always buckle her knees.

Tonight, however, her legs remained firmly locked in placed. "No problem, Carter. You did great. I was just about to go serve the food." She kept her voice tense, her shoulders stiff.

"Let me help you."

"No really, it's—"

"Carter!" A breathless female voice sounded from behind.

Gracie turned with relief. Tawny. Now she could make her escape.

Carter eased back a step as Tawny bounced to his side and possessively took his arm in hers, shutting Gracie out with a flip of her ponytail. She ducked at the last second.

"You were fantastic." Tawny batted her eyelashes. "I hope you're doing an encore."

"Actually, no." Carter tugged his arm free. "I wasn't planning on it."

"I'm Tawny Sinclair."

"Nice to meet you."

"I'm an old fan." She giggled. "But not that old."

Gracie winced at the shrillness of Tawny's laugh. "I'm going to pour drinks. See you around, Carter."

"Gracie, wait—"

"So, you're *the* Carter Alexander." Tawny's bubbly voice interrupted as Gracie made her escape. "I couldn't believe it when Gracie told me that was you. I must have somehow missed the announcement that you were coming."

Gracie hurried out of earshot of Tawny's exaggerated gushing. No doubt Carter was soaking it up. Of all the sacrifices he'd made, he probably missed the beautiful fan element of his career the most.

She stepped around two teen boys jostling for a slice of sausage pizza and joined Lori at the counter. She wouldn't be another one of Carter's groupies. She couldn't compete with those women in high school, why try now? Nothing had changed.

Gracie glanced up as another one of Tawny's crystal laughs rang across the gymnasium. Carter smiled down at Tawny, seemingly in no hurry to leave her company or the possessive hand on his arm.

Nope. Nothing's changed at all.

Chapter Five

Carter couldn't help but watch Gracie over Tawny's shoulder—which was good, it gave him somewhere to focus other than on Tawny's revealing sweater. He didn't want to seem rude, especially since she was obviously such a dedicated fan, but something about Tawny didn't seem real—not her personality or hair color.

He forced a smile as she laughed for the hundredth time, and glanced toward the kitchen just as Gracie pulled a slice of pizza free from the dwindling boxes. Those teenagers could eat. If Tawny didn't stop talking soon, they'd both miss dinner. He tuned in to her words, hoping to end the one-sided conversation.

"—back in, what, 1998? But those guys weren't nearly as good as your band. You were on your way to the top just a few years ago. I was so devastated when I heard Cajun Friday was splitting, I had to go buy waterproof mascara because—"

It seemed hopeless. The woman hardly took a breath. He needed to get out of there, fast. His stomach growled and he sent another pleading glance toward Lori and Gracie. They were both pouring drinks and didn't look up.

"Carter, my man!" Andy's voice boomed from the kitchen. "Come help me eat this last pie."

Saved by the roommate. Carter fought to hide his sigh of

relief. "Excuse me." He patted Tawny's shoulder and moved aside. "It was nice meeting you."

"Oh, I'm sure I'll see you around." She smiled, flashing a row of even white teeth.

A rush of guilt invaded Carter's senses. She was just trying to be nice. Tawny wasn't the first to blabber on in front of their favorite celebrity. She was probably just nervous. He smiled back with more sincerity. "I look forward to it."

Gracie shouldn't be jealous. She had no claim on Carter anymore—never did, if she were totally honest. Still, his attention to Tawny did unsettling things to her insides.

She focused on pouring a Dr. Pepper for Haley and handed the young girl an extra napkin. "You've got pizza sauce on your chin."

"Thanks." Haley swiped at her face and picked up her soda with a grin. "That would've impressed the boys, huh?"

"Hey, the way they eat pizza, I wouldn't doubt it."

"I think Jeremy's on his sixth piece."

"Seventh." They exchanged smiles.

"I'm gonna go dare him to eat eight." Haley tipped her cup at Gracie. "See ya."

Gracie screwed the lid back on the two-liter bottle and watched Haley flounce up to Jeremy, a high school junior who had to be at least six-five. He was the star football player. Haley was a JV cheerleader—it was the stereotypical match. They denied their feelings, but their eyes gave it away. That, and the way Jeremy blushed when Haley took the chair next to him.

Had Gracie ever been that young? It felt like eons ago instead of seven or eight years when she and Carter were in the same position—the preacher's son and the good girl who never missed a service, best friends with secret crushes. Or rather, what turned out to be a one-way crush—hers. Carter had made that explicitly clear.

Gracie shoved the bottle of soda in line with the others and looked away from Haley's charming giggle. Hopefully their story would turn out better than hers and Carter's.

"Earth to Gracie." Lori snagged one of the discarded pizza boxes and began to fold the cardboard corners. "Where are you? Mars or Pluto?"

Gracie glanced at Carter, then away. "More like Memory Lane." She took a second box and followed Lori's cue, folding the corners together to start a trash pile.

"Is it a closed tour or can I come along?" Lori grinned.

"I don't know if you'd want to. It's not pretty."

"Most pasts aren't."

Gracie blew a piece of hair out of her eyes. "I was hoping the kids in this youth group have an easier time of it than I did." In more ways than one. Gracie could relate to many of their broken homes. She had grown up without a father. Thankfully her mother had supported her both financially and emotionally, unlike many of these teenagers' current circumstances. If it hadn't been for Reverend Alexander, she'd have had no fatherly influence at all.

Lori shrugged. "They might. They might not. Everyone faces their own issues with friendships and relationships growing up." She stacked the neatly folded boxes on top of each other. "Then there are those of us who wait until we're in our twenties to get burned."

"That wasn't your fault." No one deserved the treatment Lori's ex dished out. Anger boiled in Gracie's stomach at the thought of someone cheating on her best friend. "Jason wasn't the right guy."

"Maybe Carter wasn't, either."

Gracie's hands stilled on the containers. She'd never thought of it that way, only considered herself a victim of her best friend's betrayal. What if Lori was right, and everything that happened between her and Carter was for a reason? Maybe they weren't supposed to ever be more than what they were.

She shook her head. Too much to process for now. "I need to go talk to Andy about that fund-raising idea."

"I'll finish up here." Lori opened a box to check its contents and her eyes lit up. "Ohhh, look—a stray slice of pepperoni."

"I don't know how you stay so thin."

"It's all the energy I exert getting excited about food." She wiggled her eyebrows up and down before shoving half the pizza in her mouth.

Gracie walked around the edge of the counter and snatched a pepperoni off the other end of the slice in Lori's hands. "Wish me luck."

"You're lucky I'm not fighting you for that pepperoni."

"Your support is overwhelming."

"I'm just kidding." Lori swallowed her mouthful of food. "Andy will be glad to help, you'll see. Go for it."

Gracie wiped her hands on her back pockets and looked toward the pastor, who was throwing a Frisbee with a couple of youth and laughing as it sailed over their heads. Hopefully Andy would see the cause of the gala as worthy as she did, and would be willing to let the youth group help her out—she couldn't pay them but she could offer them an amazing back-stage tour of the aquarium. Of course it still didn't solve her problem about not having a band, but one issue at a time. If the teenagers would pitch in with advertising and raising funds for the short-changed budget, she might be able to make this work after all.

Tawny breezed up to the counter, bumping into Gracie's shoulder, and grabbed a two-liter of Diet Coke. "Did you see the way Carter looked at me earlier?" Her words gushed faster than the liquid pouring into her plastic cup. "I *so* have a chance with him."

Lori coughed and mumbled something unintelligible around her pizza.

Gracie swallowed the words tightening the back of her throat and forced a smile. "Oh, really?" Maybe if she didn't look Tawny in the eye, the gorgeous brunette wouldn't notice how her heart had fallen like a deadweight in her stomach. It was no surprise. Tawny represented a slightly more mature and filled-out version of the girls in high school Carter had never been able to resist.

The memories churned faster than her stomach. Gracie

pinched the bridge of her nose, trying to ward off the details playing in vivid Technicolor of the night Carter broke her heart. A flash of green from her cashmere sweater, the neon lights from the disco ball hanging from the ceiling of the quarterback's basement, stacks of blue cups and pink punch and gold class rings. Watching Carter—*her* date to his senior party—press a varsity cheerleader into the corner of the wall with a kiss. She'd approached him, hurt covered in anger's thin disguise, until another girl's catty voice stopped her midpursuit.

"You know you're not his real date, right?"

The lights from the disco ball seemed to spin faster as Carter turned away from the cheerleader and caught Gracie's eye across the room. He mouthed her name and she stared, not wanting to hear the rest of the girl's explanation but unable to move.

The tipsy blonde continued, her words slurred but unforgettable. "He made a bet you wouldn't come with him. Not Ms. Goody-Goody Church Girl." She snorted and beer splashed from the edge of her glass. "Guess you're not very different from us after all, huh?"

The impact of the girl's words hit Gracie about the same time as the football player stumbling into her side. She caught her balance on the staircase banister and tried to ignore the lewd gaze he raked over her. "Whoa, I should have bet Carter more than a hundred bucks. You're worth at least one fifty." He leered. "Think he'll mind sharing?"

He reached for her, but Gracie shoved away and pounded up the stairs, the taunts and catcalls of the party ringing in her ears as she made her escape—Carter's laugh echoing the loudest of all.

"It's just a matter of time until he asks me out." Tawny's voice jerked Gracie from her unwanted instant replay of the past. "Hey, you all right? You look a little red."

Gracie blinked and realized her hands were clenched into fists. She drew a deep breath, willing the emotion to ease from her throat and avoided Lori's look of concern. She straightened her shoulders. "Never better."

She had a job to do—get Andy on board for the aquarium gala. The past would have to stay behind her.

And so would Carter Alexander.

Carter leaned against the wall under the basketball hoop and swallowed his last bite of cheese pizza. At a table in front of him, three high school boys wearing backward baseball caps and T-shirts laughed as they tried to see who could sink a napkin in a cup of soda first. Beside them, two older kids with multiple tattoos lining their arms finished off their dinner while discussing the youth group's limited options of dating material.

"The blonde with the braids is pretty hot." The teen with the spiky hair glanced over his shoulder toward a crowd of laughing students.

The second boy scoffed, his eyebrow ring shining under the fluorescent gymnasium lights. "That's Jeremy's girl. Everyone knows that."

"I'm not afraid of him." But Spiky Hair's eyes darted to the large football player and back. "Whatever. What about Jay-Lynn?"

"Parents won't let her date 'til she's sixteen. Got six more months."

"Bummer."

"Yeah, it stinks. Almost as much as the music tonight."

Carter straightened from his position on the wall. These guys didn't enjoy his songs? He edged a step closer.

Spiky Hair seemed just as shocked. "What do you mean, man? You don't like Carter's stuff?"

"I don't see why he had to give up the good music. This new stuff is boring. He could have been a mega star." The kid with the piercing shrugged. "I just don't get it."

Disappointment crowded the pizza in Carter's stomach. Should he approach the boys and try to explain his decision, or let it go?

The choice was made for him when they both abruptly stood with their trash. "Let's see if that Bruce Willis movie is still playing at the theater."

"Sounds good to me." The boys moved toward the trash cans.

Carter watched them wave goodbye to Andy and slip out the side doors. A late movie, in the middle of the week? It was a school night. Things sure had changed from when he was a teenager. His parents would have never let him out after the youth service, even after he had his driver's license. Maybe these boy's parents didn't know where they were—or didn't care.

He shook off the melancholy as he glanced around the gym. Several of the kids were still eating, and a few kicked a hacky sack around in the back of the room. Did the rest of them feel the same way about his music as Spiky Hair and Eyebrow Ring? He'd hoped they'd see past the sacrificed fame and into the heart of who he'd become. It seemed as though Gracie had missed that particular message, as well.

Maybe he could hang around awhile longer, bum with Andy and try to get more involved with the youth group. He didn't want his concert to be a waste. What if God had more for him at *L'Eglise de Grace* than he realized? It was definitely something to consider.

He crumpled the napkin he'd used as a plate in one fist and headed toward Andy, who had his back turned talking to— Gracie? Carter's steps slowed. He didn't want to interrupt. From the look on Gracie's face the subject was serious. But then again, how serious could it be if Haley and Jeremy were at the other end of the table? He slid into the chair next to Andy, across from Gracie, and smiled.

Gracie's blue eyes flitted briefly to his and then back to Andy. Dismissed. He ignored the sinking feeling in his stomach.

"Hey, man, get enough pizza?" Andy slapped Carter a high five.

"Is there such a concept?"

"Good point." Andy held up one finger. "Sorry, Gracie, you were saying about a fund-raiser?"

"I just think it could be really beneficial for everyone—the penguins, the kids and me—if the youth group got involved. You're always searching for a community project for them to participate in." Gracie licked her lips and Carter fought the urge to swipe a smear of pizza sauce from the corner of her mouth.

If they'd still been in high school, he wouldn't have hesitated. Probably would have licked his own finger and rubbed it right across her chin, just to get her girlie, disgusted reaction.

The difference was, in school he wouldn't have been tempted to kiss those same lips. Now, it was all he could think about. *It's not your place anymore—you missed that chance.* He shifted positions in the metal folding chair and tried to focus on Andy's words.

"Sounds fine to me, Gracie. I think a project would be great for them right now. Some of the youth seem a little restless. They need a goal, and what could be a worthier cause?" Andy tapped his fingers on the table. "You just tell me what you need, and I'll make sure we get volunteers ASAP."

"Thanks!" Gracie's eyes lit and she leaned forward against the table. "This is such a relief. You have no—"

"I'll help, too." The words flew from Carter's mouth before he could fully process them.

"You?" Gracie's brow furrowed. "But don't you have to get back home?"

Hadn't he just thought about talking to Andy about staying in town longer? What better opportunity to be a positive influence to the youth group than working side by side with them on a common goal—and if that same goal brought him closer to Gracie… Besides, maybe if he stuck around, he could dissuade Gracie from naming the wing after his father.

Carter smiled. "I'd be happy to. That is, if Andy doesn't mind having a roommate for a while longer."

"No way, man, that'd be awesome. It's a plan." Andy slapped both hands on the table. "Now we just need a sign-up sheet."

"A plan," Gracie echoed as she stood. "Right."

Carter ignored the dismay dripping from her voice. It stung a little now, but after she spent more time around the new Carter, she'd warm up to the idea—and hopefully to him.

Chapter Six

"It's been almost a week since the band cancelled." Gracie fought the urge to bang her forehead against the Royal Blend Café's wooden table. Instead, she propped her chin on her hand and rubbed her pulsing temples. "We can't have a gala without music. We don't want awkward silences."

She thought gaining the support of the youth group and Andy would make her less stressed, maybe provide enough relief to focus on the positive and temporarily forget the fact that she had no band or even the hope of one. But her wishful thinking was about as much help as her penguins at cleaning time—zero.

"Are you sure you called everyone?" Lori pinched off a piece of apple-walnut bread from the plate between them. "Surely *someone* is available in this city."

"They're not. Trust me." What was she going to do? She gazed out the side window overlooking a cozy little courtyard and fought a wave of jealousy. Patrons sipped coffee and shared pastries, talking over tabletops and buttoning their sweaters as a gust of wind threatened the napkins under their treats. Happy people, full of cappuccino and chocolate, people without the weight of an entire penguin colony on their shoulders—or the burden of an unwanted blast from the past with a certain ex-best friend.

She shifted her gaze back to Lori. "I called everyone listed in the phone book and the online directory. I even started to call the local school's marching band." She stared at the moist bread Lori enjoyed, wishing she had an appetite. Anxiety twisted her stomach in a knot that had yet to unravel. "Apparently December is a busy month if you know how to sing or play an instrument."

"I took harmonica lessons once." Lori popped a piece of bread in her mouth. "But I couldn't figure it out. Kept spitting."

Her headache intensified. "Are you kidding me? I'm having a crisis, and you're strolling down Awkward Memory Avenue."

"Chill, girl." Lori leaned forward and braced her arms against the table. It wobbled dangerously between them. "I'm only teasing because I have a great idea."

"What would that be?" Gracie squeezed her eyes shut, counting the rhythm to the throbbing behind her eyes. One, two, three, one, two, three…

"Think about it. What talented musician is in town and available the night of the gala?"

Gracie's eyes popped open. "*That's* your brilliant scheme? For me to ask Carter to perform?" Disappointment stabbed the knot in her stomach and she pushed her latte cup farther away. Other than church yesterday morning, she hadn't seen Carter since last Thursday night's concert, when he butted into her plans with the youth group. She hadn't talked to him after Sunday's service, and had no plans of rushing the inevitable—especially not to ask a favor. Besides, he probably wouldn't even do it. Not when she was determined to honor the one man he despised.

"Why not? You're desperate, right?"

"Not that desperate."

"Just ask him." Lori finished off the bread and mumbled around the crumbs. "What do you have to lose?"

My dignity. My pride. My heart—again. Gracie shook her head. "No, I can't."

"Won't, you mean."

"Same thing."

"No, it's not." Lori settled back in chair, rocking the table once again. Gracie grabbed for her cup before it toppled over. "Come on, Gracie. This isn't about you and Carter or the past or whatever memories still plague you. This is about the penguins."

The truth fluttered against Gracie's conscience. Lori was right. If the gala wasn't a success, the penguins wouldn't have their new home. She couldn't let that happen, not when she was capable of helping. They were counting on her. She refused to let them down—or Reverend Alexander. After all he'd done for the aquarium and for her, the least she could do was find a way to make this work.

Too bad Carter hadn't picked up that generous and compassionate gene from his dad. Instead, he abandoned him and everyone else he loved in one rash moment.

She swallowed the bitterness lumping in her throat and nodded. "Okay, fine. I'll ask him." He owed his father's memory this one favor, at least. Whether he realized it or not.

"When?"

"Soon."

"When?"

Gracie gritted her teeth. "Tomorrow night, after work."

"Great." Lori beamed.

Gracie pushed away from the table, back rigid. "But don't be surprised when he laughs in my face. The Carter I knew wouldn't play for anybody other than himself."

"Come on, now. He's already proven otherwise at the church." Lori's eyebrows wrinkled. "Don't go confusing the past with the present because you're still burned."

"Says the girl with the biggest scar of us all." Gracie folded her arms across her chest.

"That's different, and you know it. Jason was a mistake and I'm over it—over him."

"I'm over Carter, too." Gracie stared at the worn tabletop between them. "It's just hard to remember when the past and present keep mixing right before my eyes." Mixing like the whipped cream currently melting into her latte, though not nearly as easy to swallow.

"You're making a bird's nest out of French fries, as my granny used to say."

"A *what?*"

"You know—creating something out of what's not supposed to be." Lori flicked her straw wrapper across the table toward Gracie. "Give Carter a chance to prove himself. You might be surprised."

Gracie flicked it back. She might be—or she might be able to prove everyone wrong and be the only one right. She sighed. "I'll ask Carter about the gala and see what he says."

"He's already signed up to help with the youth group fund-raisers, right?"

"Don't remind me."

Lori's eyes narrowed. "French fries!"

"Sorry, sorry." She breathed a silent prayer for forgiveness and strength—lots of it. She might not know what was going to happen with the gala, but one thing was certain—spending time at the church with Carter over the next few weeks would be nothing short of extreme faith testing.

Knock, knock, knock. Carter jumped from his position in Andy's recliner and reached for the remote control to turn down the TV volume. "Andy, door!"

The sound of water running in the bathroom confirmed his friend was still in the shower. Apparently some things from college never changed—including Andy's thirty-plus-minute bathroom routine.

Shaking his head, he moved toward the door as the knock sounded again, harder this time. "I'm coming, I'm coming." Andy must have ordered takeout and not told him. It was a surprise the man even owned a kitchen for all the junk food he ate.

Carter peered through the peephole. A distorted, blurry image of Gracie stared back at him. He jerked away from the door, heart pounding. Gracie? Here? He looked frantically around the living room, which all too eagerly revealed the fact that two bachelors resided there. Laundry lay in a haphazard pile on the floor. Chinese-food cartons from last night's dinner were stacked on top of the TV. Empty soda cans and water bottles littered the coffee table. And the crumbs…

"Just a minute!" He swiped the wastebasket from under the kitchen sink and began to toss various pieces of trash inside. Magazines from yesterday's junk mail. The frayed piece of material he'd cut from the cuff of his jeans. Bread crust from this morning's toast.

Knock, knock, knock.

Carter tossed a soda can toward the basket, but it bounced off the rim and dripped sticky liquid on the carpet. He blotted it with a second piece of mail and then shoved the wastebasket out of sight behind the TV.

Standing, he brushed his hands on his back pockets and released a tight breath before opening the door.

"Gracie." At least he thought it was her. She wore her work uniform, but her hair was a mess—and wet? Water stains decorated the front of her polo. "Are you okay?"

She turned the corners of her mouth up, but the grin looked forced. "Huey splashed me right before I left work. I didn't have time to go home and change first."

"Huey? Must be some disgruntled co-worker, huh?"

"No, more like a very aggravated penguin." This time her smile shone real and his heart skipped like the vintage record player he'd found last year on eBay.

He swallowed the lump in his throat and stepped back. "Want to come in?"

Slowly, her smile faded. "I guess so."

"Hey, you don't have to. It's a free country."

"That's not what I meant, I just—" She blew out a frustrated breath. "We need to talk."

"Okay." He drew out the word, glancing over his shoulder down the hall. The bathroom door was still shut but he couldn't hear the water anymore, just a tuneless whistle.

"Andy, Gracie's here!" He bellowed loud enough so his friend would hear and not come out in his pajama pants. "Have a seat." He pointed Gracie toward the couch and settled at the opposite end.

Gracie perched on the edge of the sofa, white knuckles clenched in her lap. "I need a favor." Her voice shook, and she lifted her chin.

He recognized that stubborn glint in her eye. "Sure thing. What is it?"

"You know the gala event I'm hosting for the aquarium next month? The one I was talking to Andy about at the church?"

Of course he remembered. He also remembered what she was wearing that night and the way her hair curled behind her ears and—

"The band cancelled on me last week and everyone else I called is book— I mean, I was wondering if you would be interested in performing." She stared at her lap, shoulders stiff.

Despite her attempt to backtrack, he heard the truth. He was her last resort, and she was desperate. That part stung a little, but the knowledge that she needed him warmed the cold sensation sneaking over his heart. Carter felt a smile tug at his lips. Maybe his plan to stay in town to help the youth group hadn't been his own, but rather directed from the Ultimate Maestro above.

Gracie, still staring at her hands, kept talking. "The set would last a few hours, but you'd have breaks. When you're not performing, I'd have Christmas carols playing from a stereo. You could play anything mellow or jazzy or seasonal." She twisted her red hair around her finger and tugged.

Carter tried to hide his grin. She was so cute when she rambled.

"What do you think?" The hope in her gaze when she finally looked up ripped at his insides.

How could he say no? Taking the gig would not only be for a good cause, it would guarantee time spent around Gracie. The gala was obviously a huge undertaking for her, the stress was evident in the hunch in her slim shoulders. It was the perfect opportunity to show her he was different, that he was worthy of her forgiveness.

Carter met her questioning gaze, mentally kicking himself for leaving her—his best friend, and the woman who could have been so much more. What would have been different if he had stayed in Benton instead of leaving for college early? If he had stood his ground against his father and not fled for the sake of keeping the peace? He nodded slowly as the sting of regrets gave way to hope for the future. "Of course I'll help." Besides, getting the chance to be around Gracie might give him the opportunity to talk her out of the wing dedication. He had to try—if Gracie knew the truth, she'd never go through with her plans. But she could never know.

"I'll pay you what I had set aside for the original band." Gracie named the figure. "Is that acceptable? I know you're more experienced than the Creole Boys but—"

He leaned over and pressed one finger lightly against her lips. "It's just fine."

Gracie's body stilled and her shoulders stiffened. Cater eased his hand away from her face, dismay pulsing in his stomach. He'd crossed a line—he had no right to touch her. The pushing, tickling and teasing of their past was born of trust and friendship—two things he'd destroyed with his rash actions, immature behavior, and sudden departure from her life.

But the tingle against his finger indicated something else, something completely different.

Chapter Seven

Chaos greeted Gracie as she stepped inside the church gymnasium, crowded with kids, art supplies and giant pieces of cardstock. She clutched the paper bags of fast food closer to her chest as she eased around a cluster of drying posters spread on drop cloths on the floor. The teenagers were doing a great job on the advertising. Some of the sketches of penguins looked more like scarecrows, but free was free. Gracie winced as she saw another poster with barely legible writing. Maybe they wouldn't have to use *all* of them.

She ducked a marker being tossed from one youth to another and hid a grin as Haley accidentally dipped her blond braid into a can of red paint.

The girl stood with a squeal of dismay.

"Haley, breathe. It's washable." Lori hooked the teen's arm through hers and steered her toward the bathroom, mouthing the words "I hope" over her shoulder to Gracie.

Gracie shook her head. It seemed she arrived just on time. After work she'd bought burgers and fries for everyone—the least she could do for all their hard work. She dropped the bags on a table near the kitchen.

"Gracie, welcome to the madness." Andy looked up from supervising a couple of guys tracing big letters on cardboard.

"Thanks for suggesting this poster party. Sugar highs, teen hormones and paint go really well together." He winked.

"Glad to help. Let's balance that sugar with some grease." Gracie pulled several burgers from the white sacks and set them on the table. "Who's hungry?"

Paint brushes and markers clattered to the cloths on the wooden floor as the youth group stood simultaneously. "Me!"

The guys started to rush the table but a glare from Andy sent them ushering the girls ahead first.

"Looks like you're a hero." Carter's voice sounded over her shoulder.

Gracie nodded without turning, ignoring the sudden increase in her heart rate. "Not hard to accomplish with these guys."

She pulled a handful of napkins from one bag and dropped them on the table beside the ketchup packets. Lydia and Lana, the church's only set of twins, accidentally elbowed her in the ribs as they jostled for fries. "Sorry," they apologized as one.

"Want to see my poster?"

She had to turn around then, or risk being rude. Carter stood behind her, hands shoved in his jeans pockets, a boyish grin warming his expression. She swallowed twice. "Sure."

She followed Carter through the maze of artwork to a drop cloth under the basketball goal. An impressive sketch of a penguin filled one side of the white cardstock, the black feathers of the bird appearing nearly three-dimensional. The date, time and location of the gala took up the other half of the board in neat block letters.

"Wow. Where'd you learn to draw like that?"

"Come on, now. I can't tell you all my secrets."

Gracie tucked in her lower lip, trying to let the comment slide off her shoulders without effect. Tell her all his secrets? There was no immediate danger of that, not if the patterns of the past remained true. He'd never opened up the way she did—never risked his heart for her as she had for him.

Gracie released a breath she hadn't realized she held. She refused to go there now. Instead, she kept her eyes trained on the poster until the grit of the emotion passed. "It's great. Thank you."

"No problem." Carter's chest puffed a bit and he smiled. "Did I earn my French fries?"

"Sure. Better hurry before they're all gone."

Instead of rushing to the table to join the other guys, Carter looked back at the poster, his eyes holding a faraway gleam. "Remember that time in fifth grade my mom took us to the lake to feed the ducks, but forgot the bread at home?"

Gracie laughed, the image from that day tucked firmly in her memory. "Yeah, so she drove to McDonalds and bought three large orders of fries, and you ate two of them before we ever got to the lake."

"I was a growing boy." Carter bristled.

"What's changed?"

"Was that a slam on my weight?" He sucked in his flat stomach with exaggeration.

Gracie refused to give him any more compliments. "Don't even start. You know I was kidding."

"We can't all look like we did in high school."

"What do you mean? These jeans are two sizes bigger." The words blurted from her mouth before she could censor. A blush heated her cheeks and she averted her eyes to the floor, pretending to study the drawing.

"You look great, Gracie." Carter's voice grew husky and he cleared his throat. "Better than ever."

Embarrassment over his reaction and shame over having practically begged for it shrouded Gracie like a scratchy blanket. She didn't need compliments from him, didn't want to feel what they did to her heart—even now. Was she so pathetic that she still craved his acceptance?

Confusion and frustration whirled through her mind in a dark hurricane. She edged away from him. "You better go grab some dinner before it's too late."

Carter backed up a step, disappointment clouding his features. His Adam's apple bobbed in his throat. "Sure thing."

With one last glance over his shoulder, he headed to join the teens gathered around the food table.

Before it's too late. Gracie's words rang in her mind as she tried not to stare at his retreating form. "Story of my life."

Carter dipped a cold fry in the puddle of ketchup on his paper plate. He wasn't really hungry anymore, not after Gracie's sudden dismissal of his compliment. What happened? They'd been having fun together, joking about the past, and then bam—she shut down faster than a college campus on a holiday weekend.

Maybe he'd taken it too far. He hadn't meant to embarrass her, but she seemed so aggravated about her size, which to him looked the exact same as always. *Women.* He shoved another fry in his mouth. Gracie never had taken a joke well, especially not about her appearance. He learned that lesson the hard way one afternoon on Black Bayou. His parents had taken them out to ski on the lake, and Gracie made a comment about hating her bathing suit. He'd agreed, not because of the way she looked in it—he'd never paid attention to that, she was *Gracie.* He was referring to the fact that it was pink, and he hated pink. After a scalding look and two days of the silent treatment, he realized he'd better apologize, and it was a good month later before it dawned on him what had actually happened.

But his compliment tonight had been sincere. Did she not believe him, or was it something else? At least she'd seemed happy with his poster. The joy on her face had been worth the backache he'd gotten stooping over the cardboard for so long.

The metal folding chair beside him squeaked as someone pulled it away from the table. Carter twisted to see the curvy brunette from the concert sitting down with a smile. "Hey, there."

"Hi." He frowned, hoping he remembered her name. "Tawny, isn't it?"

She beamed. "That's right. You remembered."

"I didn't see you earlier."

"Just got here." She set her leopard-print purse on the table beside her. "What'd I miss?"

"A few paint spills and some burgers. Not much." He smiled, thankful tonight Tawny wore a modest button-down shirt.

"Are you singing for us tonight?" Tawny leaned forward, her elbow grazing his on the table. "I can't wait to hear you again."

"Not tonight. I have to warn you, though—if you want a burger, you better hurry. I saw Jeremy eying the last two." Carter gestured toward the football player, who seemed to be having a fry-eating contest with two other guys.

Tawny wrinkled her nose. "No thanks. I'll get a salad at home."

Carter turned up the rim of his plastic cup, hoping it would hide his frustration. Nothing more annoying than a petite woman worried about her weight. Despite her earlier comment, at least Gracie knew how to eat.

His eyes sought her out, sitting between a girl with a blond braid—the end stained in pink?—and Lori. Gracie was nodding at something they said, the burger in her hand half gone. But if Gracie had been *that* worried about her jean size, wouldn't she be eating a salad, too? "Women," he muttered again.

"What's that?" Tawny leaned closer to catch his words.

"Nothing." He set his cup down with a sigh. "We better get to work on more posters."

"Need some help?" Tawny sprang up, her dark brown hair bouncing over her shoulders. "I've got great handwriting."

"Sure, why not." Carter waved her over to his next project. He could use help on the printing—and besides, he should be nice to Tawny while he had the chance. Tonight wasn't the first time he'd noticed she didn't fit in with the others. Even the teenagers didn't flock to her like they did to Gracie and Lori. Maybe the leopard print was too intimidating.

He scooped up a package of paint pens and cast one more glance over his shoulder for Gracie. She was gathering up the fast-food trash and stuffing it into the paper bags. She looked up then, and her gaze flickered from him to Tawny and back again. Then she balled up the bags with a loud rustle of paper and turned abruptly toward the trash can.

Carter shrugged and followed Tawny to his poster. *Women.*

"So what'd you say after his comment on your looks?" Lori pulled her legs underneath her on the couch and blew into a tall mug of hot chocolate.

"What did I say, or what did I *want* to say?" Gracie tugged a throw pillow into her lap and squeezed. They'd been home from the church for over an hour, yet Carter's words still rang in her mind—along with the embarrassment of realizing his opinion still mattered.

"Both." Lori grinned and licked a glob of marshmallow from her lip.

"I just said he'd better go eat before it was too late."

Lori snorted. "That's it?"

"Yes…"

"And?"

Gracie threaded the fringe of the red pillow through her fingers and tugged in frustration. "And I hate how his words still matter to me."

Lori squealed and leaned forward, her cocoa nearly sloshing out the side of her mug. "I knew it!"

"Knew what?"

"That you still had feelings for him. He obviously does for you."

"Yeah, right, that's why he was following Tawny around all evening." The memory clenched her gut. Or maybe that was the cold cheeseburger she'd eaten.

"Did you give him a better offer?" Lori shot her a pointed glance.

Gracie shrugged. "Wouldn't have mattered."

"What's the deal with the martyr act?"

"What are you talking about? What act?" Gracie tossed the pillow from her lap, suddenly feeling warm.

"Carter's not interested in Tawny. I've seen the way he looks at you."

"It doesn't matter. He can have Tawny for all I care."

"You care. Or you wouldn't be turning red right now."

"I'm just hot." Gracie fanned at her face. "It's like a sauna in here. Did you turn on the heat?"

"Ten minutes ago you were cold, and that's why we made the chocolate." Lori leaned forward. "Quit running for a sec, okay?"

"I'm not running. I'm right here."

"You're running mentally. Just stop and hear me out."

Gracie pursed her lips and waited.

"Carter used to be an important part of your life. You guys never really got closure—it's normal for things to be weird between you."

"Thank you, Dr. Lori."

"You know I'm right."

Gracie picked up her cup from the coffee table and blew into the dark liquid. "Maybe." She took a sip, more to hide than because she was thirsty.

"Why can't you just be friends again? See what happens?"

"Too much time has passed." She shook her head. "It's too late." Much too late. How could she embrace a friendship again with the man who blew her off, blew off his entire family and hurt the one man in his life who should have mattered the most—his dad? It would be a disgrace to Reverend Alexander if she welcomed Carter back into her life—or her heart—like nothing had ever happened. She owed the reverend for all he had done for her family, and unlike Carter, she refused to mar that memory because of fleeting feelings.

Feelings she thought she'd buried long, long ago.

But there they were, creeping through the surface.

The wall clock, shaped like a steaming latte, ticked loudly above their heads, as if to punctuate her point. *Tick…tick…tick.* It counted the passing seconds, and memories, in a pulsing rhythm. Carter, standing behind her as he helped cast a fishing pole for the first time. Carter, splashing her in the Black Bayou Lake, golden sunlight reflecting off the water drops in his hair. Carter, pretending not to care when he tried to show her how to change a tire and she proved she already knew how. Always Carter, always her—together, as if they were meant to be.

Or so she'd once thought.

Lori exhaled slowly, breaking the silence. "It's never too late."

"You weren't there, Lori. You didn't feel that betrayal, you didn't become the laughingstock of your entire school. You didn't have to watch someone you thought of as a father sit and wait for his son to come home."

"It was high school, Gracie. I know it hurt, but it was years ago. You moved on. Why deny your feelings now?" Lori gestured toward Gracie's full mug with a wry smile. "Apparently you haven't had enough chocolate yet."

"I could consume the contents of an entire Godiva factory and it wouldn't change one single feeling I have for Carter."

"So you admit it! You do have feelings for him."

"Yeah, strong ones. Regret, bitterness, scorn." She glared at her friend's disapproving expression. "Don't look at me like that. I've forgiven him, okay?" *Sort of.*

"Maybe in words. Not on the inside."

"It's a start, at least." Gracie stared down at her mug. It wasn't that easy. Sure, it was only high school, but it was also more than that. Carter had taken a piece of her heart and thrown it into the choppy waters of the Black Bayou. No one had ever been able to fish it out since.

"You need to move past this so you guys can work together." Lori's voice, steady and firm, broke the silence.

"I agreed to ask him to perform at the gala for the sake of the penguins. That's the only reason and you know it."

"Yes, I know." Lori took a sip and grinned. "But that doesn't mean things can't change."

"Did Jason change?" Gracie bit her tongue at the cheap shot. Of course her friend's ex-fiancé hadn't changed. But she didn't have to rub it in her face. "Lori, I'm sorry, I didn't—"

Lori held up one hand, a sad smile tainting her lips. "No, it's okay." She squinted down at her mug. "I need to butt out. Sometimes I take my concerns too far."

"You're my best friend. You don't have limits."

"I just don't want you to miss out on something great because of a few mistakes from the past."

"I know, and I appreciate that." Gracie could kick herself right now for hurting Lori—she was just trying to help. "I shouldn't have said that about Jason."

"I'm fine."

"Promise?"

"Promise."

Gracie held out her pinkie and they hooked fingers, a silly tradition they started after watching too many chick flicks one night.

"So, you want more marshmallows?" Lori stood from the couch.

"Sure." She watched her friend leave the living room with their cups, still wishing she could take back the last five minutes of conversation. Lori was so focused on healing Gracie's past—would she ever consider her own? It couldn't be as easy as she let on to forgive and forget Jason's level of betrayal.

Or was Gracie's own faith just that weak?

Chapter Eight

"You know, the more I try to understand women, the less I understand them." Carter crossed one leg over his knee and sat back in the armchair with a sigh.

Andy laughed from his position across the desk. "Now you know why I'm still single."

"So that's the secret to sanity? Bachelorhood?"

"I didn't say that."

Big help he was. Carter gazed past Andy's shoulder, out the church-office window. A tree limb tapped against the window-pane, its leaves brushing the glass. Sunshine streamed between the mini blinds and painted stripes against the worn, carpeted floor. He'd come over this afternoon to visit Andy's office and tell him about the disastrous conversation with Gracie at the painting party. After leaving the church the night before, he hadn't been in the mood to talk. But now maybe Andy could offer some guidance. Carter might have known Gracie longer, but Andy knew this updated version of Gracie that he had yet to figure out.

"Maybe we should just forget the whole dating scene altogether," Andy said.

Carter rested his arms behind his head. "Is that what you're teaching the youth?"

Andy snorted. "Those crazy kids pair up and break up

every week. It's all Gracie, Lori and I can do to keep their alleged broken hearts glued together. You remember being that age. Would you have listened if a pastor told you not to date?"

"Point taken." Carter released a slow sigh. "I just hope I'm able to be an influence to them."

"You're doing more than you think. Just hanging around and showing you care goes pretty far with this group—it's more than some of them have ever gotten at home." Andy steepled his fingers atop his desk. "Trust me."

"Speaking of influences, what's the story with Tawny?" Carter rocked his chair back on two legs. "She doesn't seem to fit in with the youth like Gracie and Lori."

"She's a new volunteer, the kids haven't warmed up to her yet."

"Think it'll get better?"

"Maybe." Andy paused. "She's just…"

"Different?"

"Yeah. She comes across pretty strong. It's intimidating for them, I think. The guys for…well, obvious reasons, and the girls because they're jealous."

"Makes sense."

"I'm hoping Tawny will lighten up the more she's around them. They'll either break her in eventually, or she'll volunteer elsewhere in the church." Andy shrugged. "She'll figure it out. In the meantime, she's helping and we can use all the hands we can get."

"I figured as much. Tawny seems like a really great—"

A throat cleared from behind Carter. He spun in his chair, the legs landing on the floor with a solid thud. Gracie stood framed in the doorway, the sleeves of her tan and white work polo pushed up to the elbows and a clipboard tucked under one arm. "Am I interrupting anything?"

"No, come on in." Andy's smile broadened. "Have a seat."

Carter hopped out of his chair. "Here, take this one."

"This one's fine." Gracie moved the second chair closer to Andy's desk and ignored Carter's gesture. He returned to his seat, mouthing the words "see what I mean" to Andy.

Andy's face remained passive as Gracie shove her purse under her chair. "What's up?"

"I just got off work, and figured we needed to make a game plan about the gala." Gracie pulled a pen from a holder on top of the board and removed the cap. "Several of the teens last night had great ideas for fund-raisers, and I think we should act quickly before they lose interest."

"Sounds good. Lay it on me." Andy settled in his chair and folded his hands over his stomach.

Gracie glanced down at her lists. "We need to organize a group to hang the posters we made last night. Though we should probably give them another day to dry, in case it rains."

Andy nodded.

"Haley suggested a car wash to raise money for the budget." Gracie tapped the pen against her cheek. "I think—"

"Isn't it a little cold for that?" Carter leaned forward, resting his elbows on his knees.

Gracie's pen stilled. "The afternoons are still pretty warm most days. We'll check the forecast first."

"I remember the car wash the football team did back in high school." Carter laughed. "Half the cheerleading team was complaining about—"

"Let's stay on topic, okay?" Gracie's fingers tapped an aggravated pattern against the hard surface of the board.

"Sorry. I was just—"

"Jeremy and some of the other guys suggested we do a charbroil dinner or some type of cookout. They made a lot of money for the sports department at their school that way last year."

"All of that sounds workable." Andy pulled open his desk drawer and removed a calendar. "I'll check the dates and we'll get something going as soon as we can."

"What about doing something at the aquarium?" Carter stared at Gracie's profile, daring her to meet his eyes. She might be able to interrupt or dismiss his ideas, but she couldn't ignore him forever. Was the cold shoulder still from their awkward conversation the night before? The Gracie he used to know was always straightforward, honest and wore her emotions like an open book. This adult Gracie was a little harder, a little more reserved. As if she was protecting herself from something—him?

"What do you mean?" She finally turned to face him, her expression guarded.

"See if you could score half-price tickets, or a food coupon with every admission. Something to draw in the public and get them interested in the penguins. Then the fund-raisers will be more of a draw to the community."

"Good idea," Andy agreed. "It's all about marketing. That could make a big difference."

Gracie made a notation on her notepad. "I'll talk to my supervisor." She glanced back at Carter, her voice softer. "Thanks."

"No problem. I'm happy to help."

Andy's eyes darted between the two of them and he winked at Carter. "It seems like this just might work after all."

Gracie's heart thudded so loudly in her chest she was sure Carter would hear it. Not exactly the distant, removed image she wanted to convey. She straightened in her chair and willed Andy to hurry back. He'd gone to answer the secretary's phone next door.

She darted a glance at Carter from the corner of her eye. So he was interested in Tawny after all, despite Lori's projections. She'd heard them discussing Tawny with her own ears when she entered the office. Couldn't get more proof than that—not that it mattered. She had no claim over Carter's time or affection, never had.

So why did that truth bother her so badly?

"I think getting the youth group involved with the gala is a great idea." Carter's voice broke Gracie's reverie as he shifted positions to face her. "You'll have what you need in no time."

"I hope so." Gracie looked away. "I don't have a lot of other options."

"Why is it so important to you?"

"The penguins—"

"I understand about the penguins needing a home." Carter tilted his head. "But there's something else, isn't there? Is your job on the line?"

The lie would be so easy to tell. Just a simple nod, and he'd be off her case. How could she tell Carter that if she failed in the gala, she failed in honoring his father's memory? Would he even care? He'd seemed to have come a long way over the years in maturity, but the subject of his dad still appeared taboo. He had yet to mention the reverend—apparently nothing had changed in that area of his life.

Gracie opened her mouth, mind racing for a suitable response. But all she could see was the cold expression on Carter's face as he stood beside his father's casket as it slowly lowered into the earth. Death hadn't moved him—neither would her words now. She closed her mouth with a snap.

Andy breezed back inside the office. "Sorry about that. Betty's off this afternoon and I forgot I was on phone duty. I never transferred the calls to ring in here."

Carter continued to stare at her, waiting for a response as if they were still alone. Gracie faced forward, feeling his eyes bore into her profile. She clenched her teeth together and forced a smile at Andy. "No problem. We're done here."

Carter strolled down Dauphine Street, a cup of coffee warming his hand but doing little to ease the cold, lingering memory of Gracie's brush-off in the church office. He wasn't sure how much more of her drama he could take. She had mellowed a little after his suggestion to involve the aquarium in her next fund-raiser, and his hopes had risen faster than the curtain on opening night at The Strand. So why the meltdown after he asked why the gala was so important? She'd snapped that armor back in place as if it'd never slipped.

He sidestepped a small child drawing on the sidewalk and paused to take a sip of his drink. The little girl was tracing an outline of a giant flower with pink chalk, seemingly oblivious to the fact that she was about to run out of concrete and hit the gutter. A woman sitting in front of an easel a few feet away smiled at Carter before turning her gaze to the child. "Like mother, like daughter. She'll be doing portraits instead of me before long." She turned her easel so Carter could see the impressive painting of a jazz singer on her canvas.

"It's beautiful." He'd have bought it if he had the cash on him. "You're both very talented." He winked at the girl, who looked up from her chalk drawing long enough to grin.

Had his own mother seen his musical potential at such an early age? All Carter could remember growing up was hearing her predict how Gracie would do big things one day with that big heart of hers. Gracie this, Gracie that. Mrs. Alexander had also seen the truth about his and Gracie's friendship that Carter tried to deny even long after he left home. His stubborn, rebellious heart wanted nothing to do with his parents' suggestions, especially his dad's. If his father's life at the church was that full of hypocrisy, how could Carter trust that his marriage wasn't? Maybe if they hadn't been so pushy about wanting Carter to date Gracie, then maybe he would have possibly ventured that path on his own. There was no way to know now.

Heart heavy, Carter tossed his empty coffee cup in a nearby trash can. He shoved his hands in his pockets, slowing his stride to gaze up at the row of American flags adorning the front of the Dauphine Orleans Hotel. Their pristine red-and-white stripes flapped in the wind, reminding tourists and locals alike of what true pride consisted—unlike his own brush with fame that left him with a big head and an empty heart. No wonder most of the memories of his father consisted of pursed lips and a shaking head. He'd done nothing to ever earn a smile. Apparently not even keeping his dad's biggest secret was worthy of such approval.

A strong breeze lifted the collar of his shirt and Carter reached to fold it down. He couldn't change the past, but he could improve the future by making the most of the present—starting with Gracie. He'd make their relationship right, even if her new quirks and melodramatic attitude drove him crazy.

Feeling a little more optimistic, Carter attempted a whistle as he continued down the street. He'd be meeting Gracie the next afternoon after work to discuss what was expected of his performance at the gala. Regardless of which Gracie came—the old one he knew like his favorite guitar pick or the new one he couldn't quite figure out—he'd win her back. A little coffee, a little charm, a few well-tossed memories, and they'd find their old rhythm. Friendship first.

Anything more would be out of his hands.

Chapter Nine

Gracie put away the last of the cleaning supplies and bent down to ruffle the feathers on Huey's back. "Carter's going to be here in a minute, Huey. Any last words of advice?"

Oblivious to her dilemma, Huey waddled toward the diving tank and brayed once before hopping into the water with a splash.

"Thanks a lot. Some help you are." Gracie planted her hands on her hips, though she couldn't help but smile at Huey's backflip. "Show off."

He squawked again and splashed his feathers in the pool. "I know, Saturdays are playtime. But I've got things to do. Trust me, I'd rather stay here."

She checked her watch. Carter said he would meet her in front of the aquarium at closing time, so they could go over the details of his gala performance. Come in, sing, leave—that about covered it. She hoped their meeting would be as quick as possible—no need sitting around avoiding Carter's eyes and re-pressing memories of the past when she had a penguin colony to save.

Gracie gave Huey one last scratch under the chin, then wiped her hands on her back pockets. "Here goes nothing, guys." *Except maybe my sanity.* She waved goodbye at her feathered pals before securing the door behind her.

She quickly scaled the stairs out of the storeroom, pausing to tuck her hair behind her ears and smooth the front of her polo. It seemed Carter had yet to see her in anything other than her uniform—not that it mattered. She was done trying to impress him. She gave that up the night on the pier when he told her exactly what he thought of the heart she wore on the sleeve of her denim jacket.

Get a grip, Gracie. She scolded herself with every step as she headed toward the lobby door, pausing to wave to the receptionist clearing her desk for the weekend. She had to do this for the sake of the gala—for the sake of the penguins. It wouldn't be that bad. Spend a few hours with Carter, ignore the boyish charm dripping from every pore, and stick to business.

Carter waited outside the front doors of the aquarium, hands shoved into the pockets of the camel-colored jacket he wore over a pair of jeans with a rip in the knee. Gracie hesitated, wondering if she'd just walked through a time portal— for a moment, Carter looked exactly the same as he did in school, when he used to sit behind her in English and tug at her hair when he wanted to borrow a pencil, or when he'd nudge her side with his elbow and call her Blue Eyes.

He probably still had no idea what that nickname did to her insides.

Gracie drew a deep breath and stepped into the brisk, late November wind blowing in from the river. She wasn't that same lovesick girl anymore. She was a grown woman, with a mission to accomplish. Old nicknames or not, she'd get through this and do what she had to do. Besides, he wouldn't dare call her that now—he was interested in Tawny.

She lifted her chin and walked toward her past with firm, focused steps. If she had to spend time with him one on one like this, then she'd do it with elegance. Carter would never know her heart was about to beat out of her chest and her palms were slicker than Huey's feathers after a swim.

Gracie looked nervous. Either that, or she had been poisoned. Carter squinted as she drew closer, sidestepping around a young kid on a skateboard. Sweat beaded her forehead despite the cool temperature and her complexion waxed pale. Was she sick? Or just that excited to be with him? *Yeah, right. And those penguins of hers can fly.*

"Hi." She stopped a few feet away and smiled, though the effort did little to erase the crease between her brows.

"Hey, there." Carter's pulse spiked a notch and he moved closer. Besides the time she'd come by Andy's to ask him about the gala, they had yet to be completely alone together since his arrival in the Big Easy. What was the proper protocol for a greeting? Probably not a hug—she might deck him. A handshake? That seemed grossly out of place for friends with a history like theirs. Then again, their history was the reason he didn't know how to act in the first place.

He kept his hands in his pockets and hoped his expression didn't reveal his own nerves. "Good to see you. I'm glad you came."

Gracie's eyebrows arched. "Did you think I wouldn't?"

"No, I mean, I'm just glad you're here." He cleared his throat. This wasn't coming out right. "Not that I thought you wouldn't be. I mean, we agreed on the time and everything…" He mentally beat his head against the side of the aquarium, wishing he could do it for real and disappear through the glass.

"Right." Gracie's voice expressed her doubt. "So what's first?" She adjusted the purse strap on her shoulder.

To make you forgive me. The errant thought knocked Carter back a step and he faltered. "Um…"

Gracie checked the silver watch on her wrist. "I only have a little while."

"Right. Name the place. You're the Big Easy veteran here." He grinned.

Gracie shrugged, and a faint blush covered her cheeks. "Hardly. I've only been in New Orleans a few years. But I do know a spot that makes really good lattes." The wind lifted her red hair and teased curls around her face. He fought the urge to brush them back, clenching his fists in his pockets instead. That type of sudden move would only end in disaster.

Would he ever have the privilege to touch Gracie again, to offer comfort through a hug or share a joke through an elbow nudge? A thousand memories assaulted his mind, memories taken for granted until too late to do anything more than mourn the loss of them. The feel of her hair grazing his arm as they bent over textbooks in the library, the lightness of her fingers on his arm as she tapped to get his attention…

"Let's go." He offered a small smile, one that did little to ease the heaviness in his heart. *Pull it together, man. You've got to win her back to your side, not scare her away.* He could almost feel his mother beaming at them from her house in Benton, applauding his new agenda that finally matched her own—about seven years too late.

A familiar tug of rebellion pricked his heart and he shook his head to shove it away. This was different, he was an adult now and made his own choices. If he wanted a friendship— or help him, more—with Gracie, it was of his own plan, not his parents. He wouldn't let them influence him anymore, for better or for worse.

"We'll get this figured out." He motioned for Gracie to lead the way.

"I sure hope so." Gracie began to walk, not even glancing back to see if Carter followed. He ignored the disappointment rising in his throat and fell into a determined step beside her. She wouldn't get away. Not this time.

"Sometimes I think I might turn into a coffee bean." Gracie swirled the contents of her half-empty cup. "Lori and I are regulars here."

"That good of a place, huh?" Carter glanced around the crowded tables of the Royal Blend. "Their black coffee isn't bad, I must admit."

"I like it. But you have to try Café Du Monde soon."

"I've already been. It was one of my first stops." He smiled. "I actually went right before visiting the aquarium last week."

"The day you saw me?"

He nodded. "I had no idea you were in New Orleans."

"I'm surprised your mom didn't tell you."

He looked up in surprise. "Nope. I didn't realize she knew."

She nodded over the rim of her mug. "So did your dad. He helped me get the job at the aquarium before—well, you know. Before." *His death.* Even now she couldn't bring herself to say the words out loud, not to Carter's face. "That's why I'm dedicating the new wing to him."

Shock filtered across his expression before morphing into neutral. "I didn't know any of that. It was all a surprise." He paused, then traced the lid of his cup with one finger.

Alarms sounded in Gracie's brain. She eased away from the table. "Carter, I—"

"I know." He held up both hands. "I know, trust me."

"I was just going to say—"

"I know what you were going to say." Carter ran his hand through his thick hair. "Let's just talk about the gala."

Gracie stared down at her lap, the sounds of the bustling café suddenly deafening in contrast to the silence hovering over their table. They'd been having a decent conversation, why did he have to bring this up? She knew where he was heading, knew it as surely as she knew her penguins' feeding schedules and the medicine dosage Huey took for that periodic rash. She couldn't hash out the past with him right now, not while still adjusting to his sudden presence in her life.

"All right, about the gala." She let out a slow breath, trying to switch gears. "As I said, some holiday songs are required, but I think the guests would prefer a variety of other songs, as well. Something mellow, classical. Music they can talk over, though, nothing loud."

"There goes my head-banging plan." Carter snapped his fingers in pretend disgust.

Something quivered in Gracie's stomach at his smile and she took another sip of coffee to bury it. "Sorry. No head banging."

"Okay, fine, just heavy metal, then."

Now his smile was downright dangerous. Gracie couldn't help but grin back. "Just a *little* heavy metal."

"A joke!" Carter winked. "All right. We're back on track."

"Whatever." She reached over and started to pop him on the arm but stopped herself just in time, pretending to stretch instead. What was she thinking? She couldn't go back to their old means of joking around. There was way too much water under that particular bridge—she'd drown them both.

"So, a little Christmas, a little jazz. What about gospel? Off-limits?"

"Not at all." Gracie choked back her surprise. Even after seeing Carter's concert for the youth group, she still had trouble forgetting the image of Carter onstage, rocking out to secular music. This new-and-improved version would take some getting used to—if she could ever fully believe it.

"Sounds like a good lineup." Carter tossed back the last of his coffee and set the mug on the table between them. "I'll make sure you approve the final song list before the big night."

"That would be great." This *was* a new-and-improved Carter. When had he become so thoughtful, so considerate? Gracie traced the rim of her mug with one finger, unable to look him in the eyes lest her own give away her thoughts. She couldn't let him see a crack in her armor, no matter how grateful she was for his help. A crack indicated weakness, and any weakness around Carter would only lead to disaster. The last time she'd let down her pretenses had been enough for one lifetime—she had no desire for a repeat of rejection.

What if he wouldn't reject you this time? The sudden thought wreaked havoc in her ears and Gracie jumped, upsetting her nearly empty cup and knocking the coffee stirrer onto the floor. "Sorry!"

"I'll get it." Carter leaned down to pick it up at the same time Gracie did, and their gazes locked and held inches apart under the table. His soulful brown eyes stared into hers, and her breath stuck in her throat like the time she'd gotten carried away at the Holiday In Dixie jellybean eating contest. Carter had to give her the Heimlich, then teased her for a week about maybe not having such a big mouth after all.

Her fingers finally found the stirrer and she plucked it from the floor. "No, I got it." She'd managed just fine on her own these last several years, she didn't need rescuing anymore. Those days were over, condensed to nothing more than memories buried along with their junior high school pets in Carter's backyard and her own dreams of the future.

She returned to her chair with a tight smile and brushed her hair behind her ears. "Thanks, though."

"No problem." Carter shot her a wary glance but didn't push the subject. Instead, he tapped his fingers on the lined tablet where he'd been making notes. "So, I think that about covers it, huh?"

She nodded firmly, squeezing the stirrer between her fingers and ignoring the lightheaded sensation still racking her body. "Yes, I believe it does."

Chapter Ten

Gracie scrubbed a tomato stain on the countertop with a dishrag. "Why won't this come off? What's *in* this stuff, glue?"

"Use your fingernail." Lori shut the refrigerator door with her hip and moved to stir the spaghetti sauce simmering on the stove. "It dried on the surface, that's all."

"Our house is a wreck."

"It is not. You vacuumed twice—and was I dreaming this morning, or were you dusting my room while I slept?"

"It needed it," Gracie protested. "There was a dust bunny in the corner the size of Texas. I named him George."

The timer on the oven buzzed and Lori handed Gracie a mitt with her free hand. "Here, Cinderella, forget the sweeping and scrubbing for two seconds and make yourself useful."

Gracie pulled the bread from the oven and dropped the cookie sheet on the stove. "Ten minutes. They'll be here in ten minutes."

"So you said two minutes ago." Lori set the wooden spoon on the counter.

"Are you crazy? I just cleaned that!" Gracie snatched the spoon off the clean surface and laid it on a paper towel instead.

Lori's eyes narrowed. "You know, you could have said something when I volunteered to hold the next gala planning meeting here, if it was such a big deal. I just figured Andy and Carter could stand to eat something other than takeout for once. This is *your* event, after all…" Her voice trailed off and she arched an eyebrow.

Gracie drew a deep breath. "I know. I'm just a little nervous about Carter being here." In her house. Around her stuff. She released the air in her lungs with a whoosh. It crossed the line from distant to incredibly personal in one giant, unsettling leap.

Lori snorted. "Nervous? Could have fooled me."

"Thanks, Ms. Supportive."

"Anytime, Neat-Freak."

The doorbell rang. Gracie's heart jump-started as a knock followed the bell. Carter was here, back in her life—exactly where she promised herself he'd never enter again. She swallowed. "They're here."

"Are you going to let them in?" Lori turned down the fire under the saucepan.

"You get it. I'll finish this."

"It's done, except for the salad." She clicked the salad tongs together.

Gracie lunged for them as the doorbell rang a second time. "I'll start the salad. You get the door."

Lori rolled her eyes. "Chicken." She marched toward the door and pulled it open. "Hey, guys. Come on in."

Gracie ducked around the corner of the kitchen doorframe and flattened herself against the wall, salad tongs clutched to her chest. This was ridiculous. It was just Carter and Andy—an acquaintance from her past and the youth minister at her church. No reason to get all worked up.

Acquaintance? Her conscience mocked the lie and Gracie drowned out the voice by ripping shreds of lettuce from the head in the sink. She threw them in the wooden serving bowl on the counter and added a few baby tomatoes and carrots, then began to toss.

"Something sure smells good." Andy's voice boomed through the entryway.

"Thanks, it's spaghetti. We made it ourselves," Lori answered. "Eat at your own risk."

Carter laughed. "I'm sure it'll be great. Is that garlic bread I smell?"

Gracie tossed the salad faster. Who was she kidding? Carter wasn't a mere acquaintance, he was the very definition of her past, and this evening was his invasion back into her world. After years of trying to forget him, he would stroll right inside and see the sofa where she watched TV every night, the kitchen where she burned the lasagna that still clung to the inside of the oven, her beloved collection of books, the quilt her grandmother sewed before she died... It was one thing to see Carter at the church or in a restaurant, another for him to be so completely in her life—her life that, up until now, she'd managed to keep void of his presence.

"Where's Gracie?" Andy asked.

"Finishing up the salad."

Lori's response barely registered before Carter stepped through the doorway into the kitchen. "Hey, you." His voice warmed the confined space.

She gripped the tongs tighter. "Hi."

"Need any help?"

"Sure, you can carry this to the table." She practically shoved the bowl into his hands and dropped the tongs into the sink.

"Got it." He began to back out of the kitchen and nearly tripped over Lori and Andy.

"How are we doing in here?" Her eyes sparkled, and Gracie wished there was a subtle way to beat her with the sauce-covered spoon.

"Almost ready to eat."

"Great, I'll bring the bread to the table." Lori slipped past Gracie. "You guys can put your coats on the couch."

Carter shrugged out of his brown jacket as he looked around the small living area. "Nice piano." He gestured toward the baby grand in the corner.

"That's Lori's grandma's." Gracie took both men's jackets

and laid them on the end table by the front door. "She wanted it somewhere safe when she moved into the nursing home last year."

"It's beautiful." After giving the instrument one last lingering glance, Carter moved to the bookshelves by the far wall, head tilted as he perused the row of titles.

Gracie rubbed her arms briskly, feeling slightly violated at the familiarity in which he browsed her things. Did he have to touch each volume?

"Dinner's on!" Lori's announcement brought Andy rushing to the dining table. "Whoops, forgot the salad bowls."

"I'll get them." Gracie turned away from Carter and toward the kitchen but Lori stopped her with one hand.

"I will. It's no problem." She whisked by before Gracie could protest.

Gracie hesitated, then straightened her shoulders. *God, give me strength. I can do this.* She walked toward the bookcase, where Carter had pulled another novel from the shelf and was reading the back cover.

"This sounds great." He looked up with a smile. "You still read a lot?"

"When work allows." Gracie took the book and slid it back into place on the shelf. "This is one of my favorites."

"I can see why. Looks like a great story." Carter turned toward her. "I've actually been reading more myself."

"You?" The word fled Gracie's lips before she could censor. She pressed her fingers against her mouth and winced. "Sorry, you never did before. You used to say why read when—"

"When you could play. I know." Carter sobered. "I remember. But I've had more time on my hands since quitting Cajun Friday."

"What are you reading?" Carter's interests had never exceeded far past music. Maybe a biography of Johnny Cash? A Beatles memoir?

"A bestseller, actually." He rocked back on his heels.

"Oh?"

"The Bible. I've made a goal to read it all the way through."

Andy chimed in from the table, where he folded napkins under each plate. "I challenged him. If he can do it in a year, there's New Orleans Saints tickets on me."

Gracie nodded, hoping the shock she felt didn't register on her face. Carter, reading the Bible, without threat from his parents? The same Carter who used to hold thermometers to his lamp to skip church on Sunday mornings and once faked illness to get out of the service early? Christian music was one thing but reading the entire Bible—that was a commitment. She opened her mouth, then closed it. "I, uh—"

"Surprising, I know. But I told you before, Gracie. Some things change."

"I guess they do." She studied Carter as if for the first time, wishing she could see through the shell of what he used to be—the shell her memories wouldn't allow to fade. Her eyes narrowed with the effort. Was it possible that he was truly a new man? Could someone change *that* completely?

A plate clattered on the table, and Gracie jerked back, her eyes still searching Carter's for an explanation, a sign of sincerity—something concrete. *Lord, I want to believe him...*

"Get it while it's hot!" Lori's voice sounded as if from far away, yet Gracie still couldn't convince her legs to carry her away. She took a step forward, then stopped.

Carter's eyes softened and he reached out with one hand, then slowly lowered it to his side as she remained fixed in place. He swallowed visibly and gestured toward the table with a sad smile. "After you."

"So I think we're on the right track with the fund-raisers." Lori pinched off a bite of garlic bread and held it in front of her mouth as she finished talking. "We have the car wash set for next weekend and the Cajun dinner for the week after that."

Gracie shoved her salad bowl away from her plate. "Then we're into December and only two weeks away from the gala."

"Did you check with your supervisor yet on involving the

aquarium in promoting?" Andy leaned forward, his elbows braced against the table.

"The curator is all for it, and promised me discount coupons for admission. He's even going to arrange for a penguin documentary to play in the IMAX theater that weekend."

A warm rush washed over Carter. She'd taken his advice, and it'd worked. He sat a little straighter in his chair. "Which weekend will that be?"

Gracie squinted as she stared at the ceiling, as if conjuring up a mental calendar. "Uh, the weekend after the Cajun charbroil."

"Busy times ahead." Andy drummed his fingers against his napkin.

"I can't thank you all enough for helping." Gracie's voice softened. "This really means a lot."

"What are friends for?" Lori grinned. "Besides shoe shopping, of course."

Andy nodded. "It's no problem at all. The kids at the church needed a common goal. Now that our superstar's big musical performance is over, they were bound to get antsy." He shoved Carter's shoulder.

"Hey, now." Carter held up both hands. "I'm not claiming that title anymore."

"You can't deny the truth," Lori protested. "You were a star at one point, and there's no reason for that to stay past tense."

"There are plenty of reasons, trust me." *And the number one reason is sitting to my left.* He stirred his remaining spaghetti, feeling Gracie's curious gaze drill into the side of his head.

Gracie grabbed a two-liter of Diet Coke from the fridge. The spice tea Lori made for dinner had long since run out, and by the sound of the spirited conversation around the table, Carter and Andy had no intentions of leaving anytime soon.

Her sanity, however, was in severe danger of making an abrupt exit. How much longer could she sit across the table from Carter and play emotional tug-of-war? Part of her wanted to fall for his new image, to forget the past and willingly dive into the embrace of the future—a future where a renewed friendship with Carter was welcome, where his abandonment and betrayal were vague memories of another life.

The other part of her—the bigger part—knew better, and screamed danger every time her heart began to turn the other direction.

She plucked a few colored plastic cups down from the cabinet. With a smirk, she set the pink one aside for Carter. Funny how the little pieces of revenge felt the best.

Conviction struck and Gracie winced. *Sorry, Lord. I'm supposed to be nice tonight, for Your sake and for the sake of the gala.* She sighed. "Carter can have the blue one."

"My favorite color." A husky voice filled the space behind her and Gracie jumped, dropping the cups to the floor. She spun around. Carter stood in the kitchen doorway. The scent of his spicy aftershave reeled her senses and she blinked.

"I didn't hear you come in." Heart racing, she leaned over to pick up the cups.

"Sorry." Carter bent to join her.

"Do you need something else to drink?" Gracie took the cup Carter held out and tossed the rest of them in the sink. Butterflies danced across her stomach, and she reached for the bottle of soda for a distraction.

"I'm okay, thanks." Carter straightened, his eyes on her as she filled a fresh cup with ice and poured the fizzing liquid over the cubes.

Gracie's hands shook on the bottle and she tightened her grip, mentally berating herself for noticing, much less caring, about his proximity. She twisted the cap back on the two-liter and gestured with her drink toward the kitchen. "I guess we should get back, then."

Carter stayed in the doorframe. "Gracie, we need to talk."

"Nothing to talk about." She eased back a step, her heart pounding an unsteady rhythm.

"You know what about."

"Carter, forget it." She tried to move past him but he side-stepped to block her path.

"No, this has gone on long enough. I tried to clear the air between us at the coffee shop, but that didn't work, either. So just let me say it." Carter exhaled slowly. "I'm sorry I hurt you. You were the best part of my childhood and I treated you like dirt."

Tears filled her eyes in matching pools and Gracie clutched her glass of soda like a life preserver. "I concur."

"Gracie..." He let out an exasperated breath.

"What do you want me to say?" She set her cup on the counter and crossed shaky arms over her middle. "That it's no big deal? That it doesn't matter? Fine. Consider it said."

"I'm not feeding you lines, here. Be honest."

"You can't handle that kind of honesty." She set her jaw and turned away. Her chin quivered and she bit her lower lip, willing it to stop, willing her breathing to even before the torrent of sobs broke through the surface.

His gentle hand on her shoulder eased her back around. "I really have changed." His voice lowered and he reached out and traced the curve of her jaw. "Do you refuse to see that?"

Her throat tightened and a million emotions erupted in her stomach—anxiety, hope, fear. She saw it, all right. But could she believe it? She turned her head, just enough to break the contact. Carter's hand fell limply to his side.

"I'll try harder." Gracie spoke toward her Diet Coke on the counter, afraid to meet Carter's piercing gaze, afraid of what he might find in her eyes.

"I hope so." He leaned forward.

Gracie's breath stuck in her throat. Was he going to kiss her? She told her feet to move, but they remained where they were on the tile floor, holding her fast to a decision she didn't want to make. Against her will, her eyelids fluttered shut.

"You might need this." Carter's voice broke the silence and she quickly opened her eyes. He stood inches away, holding the bottle of soda he'd snagged from the counter behind her. Disappointment and relief flooded her senses in equal measure.

"If I remember correctly, you think better with caffeine, and we know Andy and Lori need all the brainstorming help they can get out there." He wiggled the bottle in front of her, a teasing spark lighting his eyes. "Plus, if I keep this, you have to be nice to me."

An unwanted grin tugged at Gracie's mouth and she finally allowed it to slip through. "I'll see what I can do."

"That's my girl." Carter stepped into the hallway carrying the bottle.

His girl. Gracie closed her eyes, pausing in the doorway before following him back to the table. She wasn't Carter's girl, now or back then—not in the way she had wanted to be, anyway. But maybe there was hope for restored friendship, a fresh start to eliminate the near decade of bitterness and regret. *Lord, is it possible?*

But would a friendship dishonor his father? She couldn't turn her back on the reverend, as Carter had all those years ago. But Carter was his son—wouldn't he want Gracie and Carter to reconcile if possible?

Confusion and doubts swarmed along with the sweet temptation to dive back into what she and Carter used to have. She closed her eyes, and a reel of memories flickered behind her closed lids like a movie. Her and Carter sharing Oreos in his mom's kitchen, laying on their stomachs in the grass by the dock and studying for midterms, laughing about inside jokes that no one else understood. Friends, like they used to be.

Gracie's eyes opened and she allowed the edges of her smile to fully bloom, accompanying the spark of hope igniting in her heart. Maybe it was possible after all.

Chapter Eleven

Carter perched on the edge of Andy's couch and lightly strummed his fingers over the guitar strings. Thankfully his hands knew the chords by heart, because he was far from focused on the music. Instead of paying attention to the upcoming notes, all he could picture was the way Gracie had looked in the kitchen. The temptation to kiss her had been strong, but even as her eyes shut, he knew it'd be a mistake—one she'd regret immediately and he'd regret in the long run. So he'd make some lame joke he couldn't remember now and ushered them back into the dining room, hoping Gracie wouldn't notice his slick palms and racing heartbeat.

He moved into the chorus of the song, humming softly. Once upon a time, music reminded him of Gracie—the nights they spent singing duets on the dock over Black Bayou while crickets chimed in harmony, the rhyming contests held on the way to catch the school bus. Gracie was always better with lyrics. But over the years, he'd managed to drown out those particular moments of the past with earsplitting reverberations. The louder he played, the further the memories stayed at bay—along with the regret.

He changed tempos as he replayed the events of the evening in his mind. The night had been decent enough, and the shared banter with Gracie gave him a brief glimmer of hope.

But the hesitancy he saw in her eyes made him wonder if things could ever be the same. They might be able to renew their friendship—recreate, possibly, but not duplicate. She wouldn't let her guard down to trust him again to that extent again—and who could blame her? She still thought he abandoned his dad.

Gracie only knew half the truth—but it was all she could know. How could he be the one to tell her that his dad, a respected minister and the only father figure she ever knew, was a fraud? A hypocrite. No, the man was dead, and along with him the hopes of a little boy searching to please his father. Time to let it all rest in peace.

Carter strummed the strings harder, moving into a faster tempo, away from the bout of unpleasant memories. But they kept coming. He closed his eyes against the music flowing from the instrument in his hands, remembering one night his band mate, Taylor Webb, elbowed him in the ribs. "Hey, who's the hot redhead?"

Carter had looked up from tuning his guitar before his band's next set and followed Taylor's gaze to Gracie, sitting in the third row of their audience in the coffee shop. She was laughing with a blond girl to her right, head thrown back and eyes sparkling even from a distance. "Gracie? She's my neighbor."

"You got a thing for her?" Taylor tilted up the last of his beer and crushed the can in his beefy fist.

"For Gracie? No way, man. We're friends." Him and Gracie? The concept felt foreign, unfamiliar—like if the Rolling Stones suddenly brought out bagpipes during a concert.

"So you don't mind?"

"Mind what?" Carter strummed his pick over the strings and listened. Finally, back in tune. He'd need to pick up another pack of strings after tonight. Hopefully the music shop on Fifth was still having that sale.

"Mind if I go for it." Taylor elbowed him again.

A lump rose in Carter's throat. "Go for Gracie? Why?"

"Look at her, dude. Why not?" Taylor's gaze raked over

Gracie from head to toe. "I'm surprised you haven't already. Or are you kissing and not telling?"

Carter's grip tightened on his guitar and he briefly wondered what would happen if he used it to bash Taylor in the head. But he had no claim on Gracie. They were friends, neighbors—he'd seen her first thing in the morning during a family camping trip, with mussed hair and drool on her cheek. He'd held her hair back when she threw up after too many marshmallows, and again a year later when she caught the flu while her mother was out of town. Gracie had no mystery to her, not like the girls who flocked their band 'til all hours of the night, eager to offer company, drinks and sometimes more to weary players after a gig.

He'd forced a shrug. "Whatever man. She ain't mine to claim."

Taylor had grinned that cocky grin, the one that usually got him anything he wanted, especially when combined with a flex or two of his muscles. But the look on Taylor's face at Gracie's polite dismissal of his invitation after the show was far better than any bashing of a guitar.

Yes, he'd been blind to what was before him then, as his parents liked to point out with not so subtle hints. Even at his father's funeral, Carter felt the pull toward Gracie as she stood over Reverend Alexander's casket and tossed a white rose onto the wooden box. Yet his pride kept him in the shadows, holding him back from doing not just what his parents had desired, but what his heart demanded.

If his father hadn't been addicted to gambling, if he'd truly lived the life he portrayed to the church and not sacrificed his family on the altar of hypocrisy, would it have cured the rebellion that claimed Carter's high school years like a cancer? Would anything have been different?

Carter's fingers stilled on his instrument and he abruptly slid the guitar back into its case. He leaned it against the far wall in Andy's apartment and moved toward the window, needing to walk, to stretch, to breathe air not tainted with the past.

Streetlights shone in the dark spaces below, casting amber pools of light across the nearly deserted sidewalks. A couple strolled by arm in arm. From somewhere down the street, a dog barked, its mournful howl echoing in the hollow places of Carter's spirit. He felt like crying that way sometimes, mourning the things that never were and now never could be.

Headlights from a passing taxicab swept past the glass, prompting Carter out of his mellow trance. He turned back toward the empty living room with a sigh. Even with Andy asleep just down the hall, he'd never felt more alone in his life.

Tuesday morning, Gracie's cell phone rang, jerking her away from the gala spreadsheet with a start. She blinked away the glare of the computer screen and fumbled for the phone in her purse, finally managing to yank it free of the side pocket. It was probably Lori calling with an update from her visit to the craft store—she'd volunteered to hunt for Christmas decorations for the gala while on her lunch break.

Gracie flipped open the cell. "Please tell me you're not buying stock in gold tinsel."

"Gracie?"

Her eyes widened. *Not Lori.* "Yes?" A flush crept up her neck.

"It's Carter. Bad time?"

"No, I—I thought you were someone else." Her stomach shivered and she pressed one hand against her waist, then frowned. "How'd you get my number?"

"Lori gave it to me. I called the aquarium's main line earlier this morning to find you, and was somehow connected to the gift shop instead. So she helped me out."

I just bet she did. Gracie forced a smile, wondering how many ways she could legally torture her best friend. "I see."

"I hope that's okay."

She let out a slow breath. She and Carter were friends, speaking on the phone—nothing wrong with that. They'd talked in stranger ways over the years. Morse code, flashlight messages—Carter even wanted to try smoke signals once but his mom put an abrupt halt to that particular scheme. "No, it's fine." Surprisingly enough, she meant it.

"Good." A long pause filled the line.

Gracie cleared her throat.

"Oh! Right. I was calling to volunteer to bring food for the car wash this weekend. I thought it only fair since you bought the last couple of meals for the youth group." Carter's voice shook slightly and he covered it with a cough.

Gracie nibbled on the end of her pen cap. Carter, nervous? No way. The Carter she knew never even got stage fright. This was the same man who once played in his boxer shorts on a dare one evening down by the river in Bossier City—and nearly spent the night in jail as a result. Still, maybe their new friendship agreement had him a little out of sorts, as well. The thought brought a measure of comfort. They were in this together. Together, somehow, they could find a way around their past.

"That'd be great. Very helpful." She shifted in her office chair, wincing at the high-pitched squeak. "We're starting Saturday morning at ten, so maybe a few dozen doughnuts and bagels?"

"I think I can manage that." Carter's voice lightened and suddenly sounded more like the boy she used to know. "You still like the cream-filled chocolate ones?"

He remembered. Gracie smiled and twirled the pen through her fingers. "Sure do. And the bear—"

"Bear claws, of course. You remember that time we debated for an hour on whether or not they actually resembled bear claws?"

Gracie smirked. "How could I forget? I won that debate."

"No, ma'am. You pulled out a dictionary for a picture of bear tracks, cheater."

"You're a Southern boy, you should have known what their prints looked like."

Carter laughed, the low timbre sending ripples of memories across the still waters of the past—this time, good memories.

This friendship thing might not be so hard after all.

Chapter Twelve

The morning of the car wash dawned sunny and clear. Gracie and Lori breathed collective sighs of relief as they set out towels, bottles of soap and tire scrubbers on a folding table in the church parking lot. Several of the teenagers milled around the empty spaces, yawning. Haley clutched a Starbucks cup to her chest as if she was afraid someone would snatch it away before she could consume a sufficient amount of caffeine.

"Praise the Lord for sunshine." Lori tied the ends of her sweatshirt sleeves around her waist. "Looks like I won't need this hoodie after all."

"It's still the South," Gracie reminded. "The weather is subject to change every ten minutes." She bent to pop open the lid of the ice chest under the table.

Andy grabbed a water bottle and unscrewed the top with a wry smile. "You mean, five minutes. Ten is pushing it."

"Okay, you realists, I'm going to be grateful anyway." Lori stuck out her tongue.

"Hmm. I think Lori here is asking to be the first to get soaked with the hose." Andy wiggled his eyebrows at Gracie.

"No way!" Lori danced away from the hoses connected to the outside church water spigots. "Don't even think about it."

"I'll do it!" Jeremy hollered. Haley squealed. He reached for the hose and Andy quickly intercepted.

"No bright ideas, gang. Cars first, water wars later."

"What cars?" Haley squinted against the sunlight, one hand rising to shade her eyes as she scanned the street in front of the church. Empty, save for a soda can that rolled down the gutter like a tumbleweed before bouncing to a stop against the curb.

"They'll come." Gracie tugged at Haley's braid. "Hopefully. In the meantime, let's finish getting the supplies laid out."

Haley took another swig from her Starbucks cup. "Just keep me away from Jeremy." The gleam in her eye suggested otherwise, and Gracie and Lori exchanged a grin over the teenager's head. Young love.

"Hey, Gracie, did you move any of the gala advertising posters we hung?"

Gracie looked back at Haley. "No. What do you mean?"

Haley shrugged. "My team hung a couple on the light pole a few blocks from here. They weren't there when we drove by earlier. I thought maybe we ran out and you rearranged some around town or something."

"That's strange. Are any more missing?"

Lori frowned. "Not that anyone has told me."

"Maybe the police took them down. Is it illegal to hang signs in this neighborhood?"

Haley shook her head. "If it is, they left all the garage-sale and lost-dog posters that were on the same pole."

"I'm sure they'll turn up somewhere." Gracie set out another bottle of soap on the table. A truck alarm honked once, followed by footsteps sounding against the gravel. She glanced up to see Carter weaving his way through the crowd of youth, two white bakery boxes held high over his head. She offered a quick wave and was rewarded with a smile.

"Doughnuts are here! And fruit, for you health nuts." Carter stopped beside an empty cardboard table to Gracie's left.

Jeremy took the top box from Carter's grasp and opened the lid. "Eew, I got the fruit box." He shoved it at Haley. "Here, cheerleader."

"What are you trying to say?" Haley's eyes narrowed to dangerous slits and she cocked one hip, ready for battle.

Jeremy's jaw unhinged and he shot a desperate glance at Carter and Andy. "I mean, uh—"

Andy shook his head quickly with a slight frown. Carter folded his arms and raised his eyebrows. A grin teased his twitching mouth.

Gracie wrapped her arm around Jeremy's shoulders before he could dig himself further in his hole. "Haley, he meant you're so thin, he figured you wouldn't want a doughnut."

"Yeah," Lori chimed in. "He was trying to be nice and give you what he thought you wanted. Like a gentleman."

Haley's lips twisted as she thought it over. A shiny sheen broke out across Jeremy's forehead, his back rigid under Gracie's arm. Gracie gave him a little shake so he'd breathe.

"Okay, well, thanks but I'm getting a bear claw." She flounced toward the other bakery box as Jeremy's shoulders sagged.

"Make sure you save one of those!" Carter called after her. He grinned at Gracie. "Or you'll have a different fight on your hands."

Jeremy exhaled. "Thanks. That was close."

"Nice save." Andy clapped Lori on the back. "You girls are pros. What would I do without you?"

"Other than stand by and laugh at the poor, misguided male members of your youth group?" Gracie laughed. "It's okay, Jeremy. Honest mistake. Just be sure to tell her later how great she looks."

Relief sagged his expression. "No problem."

"A *sincere* compliment!" Lori warned as Jeremy brushed past toward the food. "Not just words."

He threw a thumbs-up over his shoulder.

"Men." Lori shook her head.

"Hey, now, eventually we grow up." Andy gestured with a glazed doughnut. "Right, Carter?"

"I'm not getting in that one." Carter shoved his hands in his jeans pocket and rocked back on his heels. The wind lifted his curly hair off his forehead and wrinkled the sleeves of his T-shirt. "Someone might pull out a dictionary and correct me."

Gracie giggled. Lori's eyebrows shot to her hairline. "Huh?"

"Never mind. Lori, a birdie told me you liked powdered doughnuts. You might want to hurry before—"

She rushed to the food table in a blur.

"Where's my special order?" Andy threw his hands in the air. "Here I am, letting you live with me for free, for an indefinite period of time, and yet no favors. It's because I'm not as cute, isn't it?" He pretended to pout.

"Again, not getting in that one." Carter laughed. He shoved Andy in the shoulder. "Come off it, man, before I start telling stories on you."

"Stories on me?" Andy poked his chest in disbelief. "The playing field might not be so even there, my man. Need I remind you of the time—"

"Uh, guys, I hate to interrupt the masculine war here, but we have a customer." Gracie gestured with her bear claw toward a station wagon pulling into the parking lot. The sun reflected off its windows and she raised one hand against the glare.

Andy clapped his hands twice, suddenly all business. "Listen up, gang! We've got work to do. Jeremy, drag that hose over here. Luke, direct the driver to pull up near that orange cone. Haley, if you can drop the doughnut for a minute and grab that bucket of soap…"

Haley stopped midbite. "What are you trying to s—"

"Nothing!" Lori, Gracie and Jeremy shouted as one.

Haley reeled backward. "Sorry, sorry." She grabbed the blue bucket off the ground and hurried toward the station wagon.

"Ambitious idea, this car-wash plan of yours." Carter nudged Gracie in the side with his elbow.

She fell backward a step and then bumped him with her hip in return. Just like old times. "It'll be great, you'll see. They'll settle down. Beside, you're the one that brought them sugar."

"Speaking of sugar, you have a little something right there." Carter gestured toward the corner of his lip.

Gracie's fingers reached up to check her mouth.

"Wait. You knocked it onto your shoulder."

"What? Where?" She brushed at her tank and looked down just as Carter chucked her under the chin. "Hey!"

"You still fall for that! Every time since eighth grade."

"Not *every* time."

"Nine out of ten."

Gracie couldn't argue. She wiped the corners of her lips just to be sure any actual traces of sugar were gone and pretended to glare.

"Don't give me that look."

"You asked for it, prankster. Aren't you supposed to be working, anyway?" Gracie gestured toward the kids dogpiling the station wagon in an attack of arms, soap and water. The elderly couple that brought the car in stood to one side, eyes wide in alarm. Andy stepped up to intervene, then directed them toward a Thermos of coffee on another table.

Carter's mouth quirked. "They'll settle down, I believe were your exact words?"

"Eventually."

"Guess I shouldn't tell them I have a sack of loaded water guns in the back of my truck."

"No, that wouldn't be smart at all."

"I figured as much."

Gracie glanced over her shoulder at Carter's black, extended cab truck. "The back, you said?"

"Uh-huh."

Gracie grinned.

Carter's eyes widened as he realized what he'd revealed. "Hey, now, no—"

Gracie took off across the parking lot.

She was fast, but he let her win—and didn't even flinch when she nailed him in the face with a stream of water. The drops slid down his neck under his T-shirt and he puffed out his chest in mock threat. "That all you got?"

"What in the world?" Lori walked up, her shoes crunching against the gravel. "We've got three more cars over here, you guys."

Gracie tossed a second water gun to Lori, who caught it with surprise. "Cover me!" She darted behind the truck for protection and disappeared from sight.

Lori shrugged. "I'm game." She squirted Carter in the chest. "Take that, Music Man!"

Carter snagged another loaded water pistol from the sack Gracie had abandoned and returned fire. Lori shrieked and held up her hands. "I surrender!"

"Not 'til you drop it!"

"Truce, truce!" She squealed, then sneaked a shot from under her arm.

"I saw that!" Before he could retaliate, a steady burst of cold water hit Carter squarely in the back. He lunged forward and to the side, twisting around to see Gracie standing at the ready with a hose. Jeremy and Haley flanked her on each side, water pistols aimed. Lori quickly moved to stand behind them.

"What is this, a war?" Carter tightened his grip on his pistol. "Bring it on!"

"No, it's blackmail," Jeremy explained. "We want you to sing for us again at the church one night."

"We don't want, we demand." Haley raised her toy gun higher, a grin playing across her lips. "Agree, or else!"

The concerns he voiced to Andy last week vanished into the wind. They liked him—so much, in fact, they were resorting to bribery. Or was this extortion? Whatever it was, it had Gracie written all over it. He scrunched his shoulders in an effort to release the wet shirt clinging to his back and grinned at her. "Was this your doing?"

"Nope."

"It was *my* idea." Haley beamed with pride. "And we're not taking no for an answer."

"Well…" Carter dragged out the word, pretending to think about it.

Jeremy glared. "Ready, aim…"

"Okay, okay, you win!" Carter tossed his weapon on the ground. "I'll play for you guys again at the next youth service, if Pastor Andy agrees."

"Oh, he'll agree." Haley brandished her water gun. "We have our ways."

Gracie dropped the hose and brushed her hands on her back pockets. "Okay, gang, mission accomplished. Back to work—another SUV just pulled in."

The youth surrendered their toy guns and headed toward the line of cars, where several other teens had taken over the washing duties. Most of them were wetter than the vehicles.

Carter stepped forward and tucked a damp strand of hair behind Gracie's ear. Had she always looked so cute dripping wet? "So, they really like me, huh?"

"Seems that way." Gracie tilted her head to one side and tapped her chin with her finger. "Though I can't imagine why."

Carter growled. "That hose is still loaded, you know."

"So are the water guns."

"Is that a threat?"

"No, it's a promise." They squared off with matching grins.

A red sports car pulled into the spot beside Carter's truck. Tawny climbed from the driver's seat, shouldering her purse. Red bathing suit straps the exact color of her car peeked from beneath the wide neckline of her shirt.

Carter glanced back at Gracie, whose smile had vanished. She stared at Tawny in dismay.

Tawny shut the car door with her hip and slid a pair of dark sunglasses up into her hair with a wink. "So, what'd I miss?"

Chapter Thirteen

"Good thing it's not summer, is all I can say." Lori stretched her legs out against the pavement. "Or she'd be wearing even less."

Gracie shifted positions on the curb, curling her legs up to her chest. Water marks dotted the knees of her jeans and she rubbed her bare forearms for protection against the sudden breeze. "Lori..."

"I'm just saying."

Her friend was right, though Gracie wouldn't admit it out loud. She watched as Tawny squatted to scrub the tire of a midsize sedan, her knit shorts hiking farther up her thigh, and struggled to find something nice to say. "At least she's working."

"After getting here an hour late."

"She's here, though." Not that Gracie was thrilled about it, though it *was* for the penguins. But why did she have to monopolize Carter's time? Gracie and Carter had finally find their way back to joking around like old times, and Tawny's fashionably late appearance threw it all off.

"She's just working because of Carter. Haven't you noticed how she follows him from one vehicle to another?" Lori leaned back, bracing her palms against the ground.

Gracie plucked a blade of grass from a crack in the concrete and slit it with her fingernail. "I don't know what you're talking about."

"Is that code for you do know, but you don't want to discuss it?"

"Well, Carter doesn't seem to really mind her help, does he?"

Lori tilted her head to one side and studied the pair as they soaped up the sedan. Tawny flicked a handful of bubbles in Carter's direction and he ducked away with a smile. "I see your point."

"It's the way he's always been, Lori." Gracie brushed the loose grass from her hands. She'd fallen for it, again, thinking he'd be different. Would she ever learn? "Carter might have grown up a little, but trust me—some things haven't changed since high school."

They probably never would. Gracie fiddled with a stray piece of gravel, rolling it between her fingers as one incident after another assaulted her mind. Carter, canceling their plans to fish so he could go to a party with a cheerleader. Carter, calling to drop their movie date at the last minute to go see the same show with someone else, or promising her he'd be at Sunday lunch with his parents only for her to arrive and see him burning rubber out of the driveway with some blonde or brunette in the passenger seat.

The sun peeked from behind a cloud and warmed the top of Gracie's hair. She ducked her head against the glare on the whitewashed concrete and gripped the stone tighter. She'd put up with Carter's behavior then because that's just who he was, and he always made it up to her. Besides, it didn't really matter; she always enjoyed spending time with his family with or without Carter around—until the night she realized all her feelings had changed and her best friend was suddenly starting to seem like much, much more.

Her heart slammed shut against the intruding memory and she tossed the rock into the street. "That's just how it is with him. We're best friends until someone prettier strolls along and commands his attention."

Lori snorted. "You seriously think Tawny's prettier than you?"

"I seriously think I don't want to talk about this anymore."

"Fine. Then break's over, let's get back to work." Lori hopped to her feet and leaned over to pull Gracie up beside her. "No more moping. You're here to make the gala a success, anyway, not to worry about what Carter is doing. Just stay focused on the goal."

The goal—right. Gracie chewed on her lower lip as she purposefully strode toward a van on the opposite side of the parking lot from Tawny. The goal was to save the penguins, honor Reverend Alexander's memory—and aquarium contributions—and do the best job she could.

So when exactly had that goal altered to involve Carter?

Carter ran his fingers through his tangled, curly hair. "Man, I'm beat." He kicked back in Andy's recliner and propped his feet on the footrest. He needed a shower, but that would have to wait until he had energy again.

"Long day. But productive." Andy sipped at his can of Dr. Pepper from his position on the couch, ankles crossed atop the cushions.

"How many cars did we wash?"

"Six hundred?"

"I'm serious."

"Trust me, that's the serious answer my arms and back just gave."

Carter smirked. "Someone's been straying from the gym."

"Okay, Music Man, we can't all stay buff right out of college. Some of us didn't have the motivation of riches and fame to lay off the junk food." Andy leaned forward to set his drink on the coffee table.

Carter grinned and reached for the remote control on the end table. "Guess that means I'll have to be careful now that I'm a nobody again."

"Do you ever wonder if the world will let you be a nobody again?" Andy punched the couch pillow under his head into submission. "I always thought once famous, always famous."

"Guess we'll find out." Carter shrugged as he flipped channels. Weather, local news, CNN. "That's why I want to get involved with good causes while I still have some influence."

"You were a big hit today. I heard about the water war bribery to get you to do another concert." Andy laughed. "Those crazy kids never fail to surprise me."

Carter turned down the volume and shifted in the recliner to better see his friend's face. "So you're okay with me singing for them again?"

"Sure, whenever you want. We're all a little gala-focused right now, so the rest of the youth-group calendar is pretty clear outside of these upcoming fund-raisers."

"I'll plan on it, then. Did we make good money today?"

"Gracie and Lori took it home to count. I imagine we pulled in maybe two hundred dollars in donations."

"That's great."

"Yeah, not bad. The Cajun charbroil is next. How's your grilling ability?"

"About the same as your singing ability." Carter ducked the pillow Andy threw.

"Thanks for the warning. We'll figure something out. If all else fails, we'll just bury everything in spices."

"That's how you people eat down here, anyway, isn't it?"

Andy aimed another pillow. "Careful. Now you're dissing my home turf."

"You know I'm kidding. I'm really starting to enjoy this city."

"Then why not hang around indefinitely?"

"You that lonely?" Carter threw the pillow back at Andy.

"Ha, ha." He caught it and shoved it behind his head. "Just a thought. I know certain people would be happy to see you stay."

"So you noticed Gracie warming up to me, too?" The day had gone very well—nothing had shocked him more than Gracie taking off toward his truck and the water guns like that. Carter grinned at the memory. She was finally lightening up, reminding him more and more of the old Gracie, the one who used to be his right hand, his teammate, his bud—

"Uh, I was actually talking about Tawny."

Carter clicked off the TV. "Are you serious?"

"I think Tawny's got a crush."

"A crush?" He threw back his head and laughed. "You've spent too much time around your teenagers, man. This is the real world of adulthood—there are no crushes or going steady or wearing letterman jackets."

"I'm not kidding. Tawny has always been somewhat of a flirt but she seems really interested this time."

Carter's brow furrowed. "I was just helping her wash the bigger cars. I didn't mean to give her that impression."

"You're a rockstar, dude. You ooze impression."

"Did I flirt back?"

"Maybe not intentionally, but Gracie thought so."

"She told you that?" Carter straightened in the recliner so fast his head spun.

"Not in so many words. But you forget I watch this stuff in my youth group every week, all year long. I can tell when a girl is jealous."

"That's crazy."

"Hey, it's not a gift I wanted, but I got it."

"Not that. I meant it's crazy that Gracie would be jealous. We're just now starting to find our friendship footing again."

"Exactly. You're unestablished, you're in relationship limbo. Don't you ever read?"

"Apparently not the chick books you've been reading." Carter yanked the recliner handle and his feet dropped to the floor with a thud.

"They're not chick books, they're relationship guides." Andy shrugged. "I don't want to stay single forever, you know."

Carter leaned forward, bracing his elbows on his knees. "So you're saying what, specifically?"

"I'm saying be careful."

"With?"

"Both of them." Andy shook his head with a shudder. "I don't want to be on the counseling end of either of their broken hearts."

Chapter Fourteen

"Do you think there are shoes in Heaven?" Lori trailed her finger over a pair of red polka-dot sandals and released a wistful sigh.

Gracie shifted her shopping bag to her other arm and shrugged as she glanced around the colorful boutique. Jewelry and various accessories lined the display tables around stacks of shoes, tops and purses, all decorated with piles of fluffy fake snow and red holly berries. "Good question. Do we walk the streets of gold barefoot, or in designer duds?"

"Hopefully we get a vote." Lori moved toward a table, where a miniature sleigh pulled a display of discounted shoes, and picked up a pair of tall black boots. "Oh! These Madelines are on sale!"

"Cute." Gracie checked her watch. Almost noon. They could grab a quick lunch at Rocky's before completing the rest of their errands for the gala—that is, if she could pry Lori away from the boutique. The hot pink sign out front had lured her in like a crawfish to a net.

"Cute? I was thinking more like stunning." Lori turned the boot over. "I wonder if they have a size nine."

"I'll get a sales clerk." Anything to hurry her along. Gracie made her way toward the counter at the back of the store, where a curly-haired brunette waited behind the register. "My friend would like to try on a pair of boots, please."

"Gracie, what are you doing here?" A voice sounded over her shoulder.

She turned at the familiar sound, dismay inching up her spine. Tawny Sinclair stood next to a display of T-shirts, a frown marring the edges of her plumped, glossy mouth. She smoothed her fitted top over the waist of her trousers and arched a painted brow. "I didn't know you shopped here."

"Hey, Tawny. This is our first time." Gracie gestured toward Lori, who was pivoting in front of a display mirror with a gold purse tucked under her arm. "Lori saw the sign out front, and well—"

"I see." Tawny's gaze swept the length of Gracie and she smiled, but it didn't quite reach her eyes. Gracie suddenly wished she'd worn something dressier than jeans and a sweater. But that was silly—it was Monday, her day off, and she had the right to be comfortable while she shopped. She had no one to impress.

Gracie turned back to the salesclerk. "My friend needs a size nine in the black Madeline boots, please."

"Certainly." The salesclerk hurried to Lori's aid, looking relieved to be dismissed from the mounting tension.

Gracie wished she didn't have to turn back around and face further potential embarrassment. But Tawny needed prayers, not rudeness. She eased around with what she hoped passed for a sincere smile. "Missed you at church Sunday."

"Oh, I was there, I stayed in the youth department to help out. One of the other volunteers was sick." Tawny picked up a black T-shirt with a fleur-de-lis imprint and held it in front of her chest. She squinted in the mirror. "I did, however, see you sitting with Carter during the service."

Aha. So that explained Tawny's attitude. Carter had sought Gracie out during the opening hymn, and slid into the end of the pew before she could protest or decide if she wanted him to.

"Yeah, we sat together." She stole a sideways glance at Lori, wishing she would come to her rescue with some witty comment. If anyone could get rid of Tawny, it'd be her best friend. "So?"

"So," Tawny hissed, dropping the shirt back in the pile, "what's going on with you and him?" She stepped closer to Gracie.

"Nothing really. We're friends." *Sort of.*

"What's with the *really* part?"

"I don't know." She fought the urge to step backward, away from Tawny's questioning.

"How can you not know? Either you're together or you're not." Tawny pressed forward. "Which is it?"

"Why do you care, Tawny?"

She reeled backward. "I don't. Trust me, if I wanted him, he'd be mine by now." Tawny smirked, but uncertainty clouded her overly made-up eyes.

"We're just friends. So there isn't a problem." Gracie reached for a sandal on the table nearest her, not loving the zebra print but desperate for a distraction—and something to do with her shaky hands.

Tawny's shoulders relaxed and she fumbled in her purse. "I guess not, then. Hey, did you hear we're having the next ad campaign party for the gala at my house?" She pulled out a business card with her address. "I confirmed with Andy this morning. I wanted to contribute, so we'll be making the plans for the Cajun charbroil at my condo this Wednesday night around six-thirty."

"Is the youth group coming, too?" Gracie took the card and shoved it in her back pocket, fighting the urge to wipe her fingers in the process. Hopefully Tawny's cattiness wouldn't rub off on her.

"I'm sure some will. I'm bringing deli sandwiches for everyone." She tossed back her hair, her gold earrings catching the light. "It'll be fun."

An evening with Carter, on Tawny's turf. "Oh, yeah, a blast."

"She actually said that he'd already be hers if she wanted him?" Lori took a bite of crawfish pizza, cheese stringing from her mouth. She wiped the excess around her finger and pulled it free. "I had no idea she was so tacky—and after all you've done for her."

"Trust me. If tacky was a town, she'd be the new mayor." Gracie stabbed her pasta salad with her fork, then sighed. "I shouldn't let it bother me. Who cares if she likes Carter?"

"She's never been like this about other guys before. I guess Carter has her all stirred up."

"I'm thinking it's mutual." Gracie glanced around the crowded pizza parlor. Thankfully none of the other patrons were within hearing distance of their table.

"You don't know that for sure." Lori reached for her cup of soda, the ice clinking as she tilted the glass.

"I think the car wash was proof enough."

"Proof of her interest, maybe—not necessarily his."

"I thought I was finally okay with the idea of being Carter's friend again, but it's like the past won't completely go away—and seeing Tawny today just brought back all these others emotions that are still there."

Lori crunched a piece of ice, head tilted as she thought. "If it were me, I would have to decide if being with the guy was worth the drama."

"*Friends* with the guy, you mean."

"Whatever."

"Worth the drama, huh?" Gracie brought a piece of pasta to her lips, then set her fork back on her plate. She wasn't hungry anymore—Tawny had sufficiently ruined her appetite. "How would you decide that?"

"I think it would be decided for me." Lori reached for another slice of the pie between them. "True love rarely gives us a choice. And if it wasn't true love, then…" She stuck the pizza in her mouth and shrugged.

True love? They were just talking about her and Carter being friends. Yet the words struck a chord she couldn't ignore. Did she still love Carter, despite everything he'd done? Everything she'd lost? It was too much to process, especially when she wasn't even sure if she could handle being his friend again.

STEEPLE HILL BOOKS,
publisher of inspirational romance fiction, presents...

Love Inspired®

A SERIES OF CONTEMPORARY
LOVE STORIES THAT WILL LIFT YOUR
SPIRITS AND WARM YOUR SOUL!

GET 2 FREE BOOKS!

2 FREE BOOKS

TO GET YOUR 2 FREE BOOKS, AFFIX THIS PEEL-OFF STICKER TO THE REPLY CARD AND MAIL IT TODAY!

Plus, receive two
FREE BONUS GIFTS!

GET 2 FREE BOOKS!

Love Inspired

YES! *Please send me the 2 FREE Love Inspired® books and 2 FREE gifts for which I qualify. I understand that I am under no obligation to purchase anything further, as explained on the back of this card.*

affix free books sticker here

☐ I prefer the regular-print edition   ☐ I prefer the larger-print edition

113-IDL-EYSY   313-IDL-EYTN   121-IDL-EYTC   321-IDL-EYTY

FIRST NAME   LAST NAME

ADDRESS

APT.#   CITY

STATE/PROV.   ZIP/POSTAL CODE

Steeple Hill®

Gracie gazed past Lori's shoulder toward the open kitchen in the back of the restaurant. Chefs worked in harmony, tossing pies in the air, smearing sauce, sliding the giant white piles of dough into large ovens. Their steps were carefully orchestrated, their system perfected—everything had a particular order.

No wonder You like for us to follow Your plan, Lord. Gracie watched a worker in a large apron slide a delicious-looking pizza from one of the ovens. *If we mess up the order of the steps, we won't be as successful.*

Carter obviously hadn't followed that plan and deferred from God's path, choosing the pleasure of the world over the teachings of his childhood. It was what had ultimately driven them apart—not the other girls, the music, the pranks he pulled or the scars he left—but the difference in their hearts.

Besides the fact he up and left after she bared her soul.

She tapped her fork against her plate. Lori was right. Gracie had to decide if being friends with Carter now was worth forging through the pain of the past—and the consequential emotions that the wounded high school girl part of her heart couldn't forget.

Chapter Fifteen

Gracie dunked another chip into the bowl of salsa and cupped her hand under it to catch any spills. She crunched loudly, hoping to drown out the sound of Tawny's giggle as she fawned over Carter. Did the girl never quit? If Carter wasn't interested, then he sure was good at pretending, laughing at Tawny's ridiculous jokes and helping her in the kitchen.

Or like now, as they stood by the fireplace, Carter's arm braced against the mantel. He smiled down at Tawny, shaking his head when she offered him yet another sandwich. Did she think he wasn't capable of fixing his own plate? Gracie chewed louder. She should have expected this. She *had* expected it, actually, just hoped to be proven wrong. Carter would always be Carter in the presence of a pretty woman—it was in his genes.

"Do you get the feeling you're being watched?" Lori whispered as she leaned past Gracie toward the bag of chips on the coffee table.

Gracie stopped chewing and glanced around. The kids from the youth group were gathered around the kitchen table in the adjoining dining room, scarfing down the last of the deli meat. Andy sat across from them in a brown settee—rather uncomfortably judging by the pinched expression on his face—

his attention riveted by the church calendar in his lap. The only things staring back at Gracie were the numerous African animal figurines that took over every spare inch of Tawny's living room. A giraffe posed as an end table. Monkeys scampered up a lamp on the floor-to-ceiling bookshelves and a herd of zebras stood guard over the fireplace mantel. A porcelain leopard prowled under the orange striped curtains. "Actually, now that you mention it…"

"This place creeps me out."

"It's elegant, I guess. If you like this style." Gracie plucked another chip from the sack. Better to focus on Tawny's unique interior designing than the way she ogled Carter like a lioness on the prowl.

"I thought we were here to make plans for the Cajun dinner." Lori sat back on the sofa and crossed one leg over the other.

"I think we're here for Tawny to have a home-field advantage."

"What do you mean?"

"Apparently we're fighting over the same guy."

"Carter?" Lori frowned. "I thought you said you weren't interested in being more than friends."

"I'm not. She's the only one doing the fighting."

"This is ridiculous." Lori stood up and cupped her hands over her mouth. "Hey, guys, you done eating? We need to get started."

The kids mumbled in protest around the food in their mouths.

"Okay, then, chew while you listen. Pastor Andy? The floor is yours." Lori bowed and returned to her position on the couch.

"Thanks for keeping us on task, Lori." Andy held up the calendar. "Okay, the Cajun dinner is scheduled for this Saturday. Is everyone here planning to attend?"

Heads nodded.

"Who wants to volunteer to bring what? We can use the church grill and barbeque tools. But we need food and desserts. Any suggestions? Remember, this is supposed to be Cajun."

"What about bread pudding?"

"I can bring a King cake."

"You bake?"

"No, silly, my mom does."

The teens jabbered off various suggestions. Gracie listened, proud of them for stepping up and getting involved. She should do something to thank them publicly at the gala—they more than deserved it.

Movement from the fireplace drew Gracie's attention. Carter's arm slid from the mantle and relaxed at his side as he turned away from Tawny, folding his arms casually over his chest. He caught Gracie's eye and smiled, and she urged the corners of her mouth up in return. Fake it 'til you mean it— that'd be her new motto. There was no use letting Carter know she was bothered by his interest in Tawny—it'd only urge the other girl on and create more complications in Gracie and Carter's fledging friendship.

Too late. Tawny followed Carter's gaze and her eyes narrowed. She stepped closer to him and frowned at Gracie.

You don't care, you don't care. The chant straightened Gracie's spine and she forced a little more brightness into her smile. She kept up the inner monologue as she turned back to the discussion. At least her mind was on the right track.

Maybe her heart would catch up in time.

Carter snagged a brownie from the plate on the coffee table, almost dropping it in surprise when he realized the glass top was held up by a black panther. What was with this safari room? Apparently Tawny's interest in animal print went behind that purse she toted everywhere. Subtle, she was not— in taste or in the way she came on to him.

Andy's words from the other day were starting to make sense. *Tawny has always been somewhat of a flirt, but she seems really interested this time…*

Carter didn't want to hurt or embarrass her, so he tried to

listen as Tawny spouted various memories of his old concerts, but the truth was he couldn't keep his eyes from Gracie. She sat on the couch by Lori, shoveling chips into her mouth as if the world was coming to an end—and what was with the fake smile? What had he done this time? The woman turned hot and cold like a faucet.

Tawny's constant attention didn't really allow him the opportunity to find out what was bothering Gracie, but knowing the woman's hesitant position in the church, how could he put Tawny off? Besides, he was starting to get the impression she didn't like *him* so much as the rockstar image he used to represent.

He bit into the brownie, wishing there was a way out of this situation. He was through breaking hearts. The only one he wanted sat right across from him, marking in a notebook as Andy went through the details of the upcoming weekend fund-raiser. How could he show Gracie that he wanted to make this new friendship with her work—without being rude to Tawny in the meantime?

Feeling someone's eyes roving over him, he turned slightly. Tawny watched him from the loveseat, legs crossed and one high-heeled shoe dangling off her foot. A slow smile seeped over the edges of her mouth, and her lips parted slightly. She quirked an eyebrow.

Carter quickly reached for a second brownie. He recognized that look, that body language—it was the same invitation he'd received too many times to count from groupies after concerts. Those days were over, and he wasn't about to relive them now. He needed a plan, fast.

Andy wrapped up his comments with a tap on his calendar. "Any more questions, see Gracie. Volunteers for food, talk to Lori. They've got the lists. Thanks guys!"

Carter stood, and so did Tawny. He sidestepped around the coffee table and moved to the arm of the couch beside Gracie. "Need a hand?"

She looked up, surprise lighting her blue eyes. His breath caught, and he brushed brownie crumbs off his fingers onto his jeans, desperate to break the eye contact. How did she do that with one look? If he weren't careful, she'd have him spiraling out of control faster than the Tilt-A-Whirl they used to ride at the state fair. Already the line blurred between friendship and more.

"I've got it under control, but thanks." She offered a slight smile and glanced back at her notepad.

Carter sat on the arm of the couch and leaned over her shoulder. Her perfume tickled his senses and he exhaled abruptly. "Let me know if I can help bring anything Saturday."

From the corner of his eye, he saw Tawny freeze in the middle of the living room, her gaze riveted on them. Then she turned and whisked up the brownie plate in a huff before disappearing into the kitchen. His shoulders loosened.

"I'll let you know." Gracie twisted to face him. "But you've already done plenty, bringing the snacks for the car wash, painting posters and singing at the gala."

"Speaking of which, I have the song list ready for your approval."

"Great. Just bring it Saturday morning."

Tawny peered at them from around the kitchen doorframe, and Carter drew a deep breath. He had to do something before Tawny got the wrong impression about his intentions, and before Gracie wrote him off completely. He closed his eyes briefly. "Actually, I had another idea."

Chapter Sixteen

Carter waited outside the New Orleans Court Building on Royal Street, squinting against the late afternoon sun streaming through nearby tree branches. In his hurry to meet Gracie, he'd left his sunglasses at Andy's.

He turned a half circle on the sidewalk, searching the Friday crowd for a hint of Gracie's red hair. He'd asked her to meet him here to go over the song list for the gala, and he had a surprise up his sleeve, as well—a walking tour of the city. The tourist crowds, the rich foods and the exercise should make for a fun day, and hopefully in the open atmosphere, Gracie wouldn't feel so intimidated by their developing friendship. He was determined to cover a lot of ground today—in more ways than one.

Carter checked his watch. She should be here any minute. He peered up at the expanse of the white court building before him, taking in the impressive marble detail and the shuddered windows. A walking tour brochure he'd snagged informed that the gigantic structure held the Louisiana Wildlife Museum and the Circuit Court of Appeals for the Fifth District.

He folded the pamphlet and tucked it in his jeans pocket, wondering if he could use any of the trivia facts to impress Gracie. Being as enamored with the city as she was, she probably already knew half of them.

"Hey, there." Gracie's soft voice sounded from behind, and he quickly turned.

"Hi." Carter tried to keep the relief from his tone, but nothing could control the grin breaking across his face. She came. And she looked great, with her hair shoved into a carefree ponytail and a denim jacket folded over one arm. She'd changed from her work uniform into a pair of flowing brown pants and a blue top that brought out her eyes. He shoved his hands in his pockets so he wouldn't pull her into a much-needed hug. "You hungry?"

"Starving." She glanced up at the court building, then back at Carter. "Uh, why did you want to meet here to go over the song list again?"

"I wasn't completely honest with you."

Her eyes narrowed and he rushed ahead before she could place too much negativity into that sentence. "I heard of a self-walking tour we could take while we discussed the gala. I thought it might be fun—plus, with you being the *N'awlins* expert, we could skip the boring parts and see the fun places." Carter drawled the southern slang with a wink, hoping to erase the crinkle in her brow.

Gracie's expression relaxed and she even laughed. "Sounds good to me, if you promise not to talk like that again. What's supposed to be stop number two?"

Carter checked the brochure. "Casa Faurie, further down on Royal. It was a mansion, but now it's—"

"Brennan's Restaurant, I know." Gracie slid her arms into the sleeves of her jacket. "It's a neat place, they have an amazing outdoor dining patio. But probably too expensive—their steaks are some of the best around."

"Dinner's on me, don't worry about it. We can eat there or anywhere else you'd like." He ushered her forward, grateful that he actually had the funds to be able to make such a promise. At least there were a few positive benefits to his old life.

Gracie's feet remained planted on the sidewalk and her eyebrows arched. "Carter, I don't—" She stopped, and looked down at their feet as if weighing her words.

She thought it was a date. He pushed down the wave of un-identified emotion clogging his throat—no time to process that now—and pasted on a carefree smile. "Come on, can't a friend buy another friend dinner?"

She chewed on her lower lip, mulling it over. Then she sighed. "Okay, if you're sure."

Oh, he was sure. If only she'd let him prove it. For one chance at her forgiveness, he'd buy her the moon if it were for sale. He nodded and extended his arm. "Positive."

"In that case…" She smiled and wrapped her hand around his elbow, and his stomach clenched at the contact.

They began to walk.

"I guess I shouldn't be surprised. You have money from Cajun Friday, don't you?"

"A little." Carter kicked at a rock on the sidewalk. "I'm trying to do the right thing with it, make investments. Be smart, you know."

"Buy expensive steaks."

Carter laughed. "That, too."

"Your dad would be impressed, I'm sure. He always seemed to handle his finances so well—tithing, donating to charities and good causes… I think God blessed him for it, you know? All that money he made as a stock broker before his pastoral career."

Carter swallowed. "Right."

"I'm serious. I bet he'd be proud of you."

"Better late than never I guess." Carter abruptly released Gracie's arm, the wind suddenly chilling him through his long-sleeved T-shirt and pullover. He hated the bitterness in his words, but felt incapable of concealing it. He didn't want to get into this right now. If he looked Gracie in the face, she'd know the truth, see it in his eyes. He couldn't ruin his father's reputation—not on such an innocent day, when things were going so well.

Gracie stopped walking and moved in front of him, forcing eye contact. "Carter, what do you mean? Your dad loved you."

Carter looked away, toward the sun-drenched branches of

the trees next to the court building. Words churned in his mouth, and he kept his lips pressed together, afraid of letting the wrong ones free.

Gracie waited, the breeze whipping wisps of hair free from her ponytail. She tucked them behind her ears, and Carter wished he had the right to do the same. Their friendship would never get back to normal if he didn't explain something. She needed—no, deserved—an answer.

He considered his words carefully. "My father had high expectations of me, expectations I never met. He wasn't proud, Gracie. I gave him nothing to be proud of."

She opened her mouth as if to argue, then snapped it shut. The simple motion rocked Carter's stomach. The truth was evident in the firm line of her mouth—he had wasted the majority of his life and she agreed. What father could be proud of broken curfews, beer cans in the flower bed and rock and roll?

And who better to remind him of his faults than Gracie?

Memories of comments past bombarded his mind. His mother, saying how wonderful Gracie was to volunteer in the nursery. His dad, going on and on about what a good kid Gracie was, how she never came home drunk or caused her parents stress. *Gracie's so sweet. Gracie's perfect for you. Gracie could straighten you out...* Well, Gracie's mom hadn't lived a double life and expected her daughter to keep her secret. Maybe it'd have been easier to stick around more if—he mentally clamped his hand over his mouth before he said too much, even to himself.

"Listen, it doesn't matter. We should be heading toward Brennan's, not standing here stuck in the past." Carter took Gracie's hand. Her confused expression softened his heart and erased the momentary replay of bitterness. He traced a line in her palm, finding the scar from the time in second grade when she fell from the swing and cut it on broken glass. The wound had healed but the jagged imprint remained—like Gracie's impression on his heart.

He met her eyes and tucked her hand safely into the crook of his arm. "I'm much more interested in the future."

* * *

Gracie peered up at the Maison Seignouret house before her, the impact of the elaborate three-story mansion lost in the lingering sensation of Carter's touch. How did he stop such an important conversation with a single brush of his fingers? Worst of all, why did she let him? She shouldn't be so weak, so easily distracted—but every moment with him seemed to make up for lost time. She wanted to embrace the Carter she knew now, and try to put the old Carter out of her mind once and for all.

If only she could figure out his intentions toward Tawny.

Gracie forced the negative thoughts away and turned to study the fan-shaped, iron *garde de fries* on the side of the structure's top story. *It doesn't matter, we're just returning to friendship. Nothing more.*

"It says here a merchant named Francois Seignouret built this house in the 1800s." Carter pointed to the brochure, then craned his head as he looked up at the mansion. "Supposedly he had a thing for putting *S* designs into his work. You're supposed to be able to see one over there in the grillwork." He pointed.

"I can't find it." Gracie tilted her head, eyes searching the front of the building. She stood on tiptoe to peer above the head of a passing tourist. "Where?"

"There." Carter leaned down, pressing his head beside hers, and gently moved her chin. "See?"

She followed his gesture, trying to ignore that his proximity made her breathless, and finally made out the famous design on the side of the massive structure. "How beautiful."

"Very." Carter eased away, his eyes never leaving hers.

The flush from earlier turned into a flaming heat that crept up her chest and toward her ears. Did he realize the pain his words caused her heart? Or was he just kidding around? She couldn't tell anymore, couldn't decipher the nuances of this older Carter. He thought she was beautiful—but if that were true, where did Tawny come into play? Was he just dishing out compliments to all the women in his life? She didn't want to take that role again, to be the girl he focused on only when no one else was around.

Her shoulders stiffened. "Ha, ha. Funny."

Hurt flickered across Carter's eyes. "What is with you and compliments?" He ran a hand through his hair in a frustrated gesture. "I'm being serious. It wasn't a joke."

"Just forget it." She turned back to study the Seignouret house, but the entire structure blurred before her in a wave of tears. Why did she have to ruin such a good day with her stupid emotions? Would the past ever let her go? The laughs of the students from school echoed in her ears, a constant reminder that she wasn't good enough for Carter, wasn't what he wanted. She was Gracie, the naive goody-goody who actually believed once that her best friend could love her back. She'd made every effort she could to show him that, yet all she had really convinced him to do was leave. Had the offer of her love been so terrible?

"Are you crying?" Carter's voice jerked her from her reverie and she quickly wiped at her eyes as embarrassment reared its ugly, all-too-familiar head.

"Come here." Carter took her hand and led her away from the crowd toward St. Louis Street. He stopped in front of a bench across from Antoine's Restaurant and tugged her down beside him.

"What is it? What did I do?"

Gracie shook her head, her throat clenched into a ball. She couldn't speak if she wanted to, and she had nothing to say. She refused to bring up the past again—he'd already apologized. How would they ever develop their new friendship if she couldn't release the old one?

If that's what she even wanted. Maybe letting go completely would be easier. The tears pricked her eyes and she blinked rapidly, determined not to lose control.

He reached over to smooth her hair behind her ear. "Gracie, I've missed you, you know that?"

The inside of her mouth suddenly felt like a wad of cotton, despite the jumbo lemonade he had purchased for her two stops ago. She cleared her throat. "You have?"

"I never stopped thinking about you."

Disbelief swirled in a foggy cloud. He was toying with her, had to be—otherwise, why now? What had changed? She shifted away from him on the bench, her heart pounding as rage and hope battled for control. "Carter, you can't just come back into my life after abandoning me and expect one afternoon of hanging out to clear everything up." Oh, how she wished it were that easy. But there were too many years of silence, too many months of tears, anger and pictures cut into a zillion pieces to pretend otherwise.

Carter fell heavily against the back of the bench with a huff. "What do you want me to say, Gracie? I've tried everything I can think of to apologize for hurting you, and it's not enough. It's never enough."

"Trust me, I understand the feeling." She rolled her lower lip between her teeth, hoping the action would stop the torrent of hurtful words threatening to pour out. *Oh, God, why did I have to ruin our fun afternoon with this?* They'd toured the city, admired an Elvis impersonator's antics, elbowed and joked as if they were still in high school. They'd laughed at a storefront's fat Cajun Santa, who wore a swimsuit and tank top and whose sleigh was pulled by eight tiny crawfish.

During the evening, she'd caught glimpses of the man Carter had become in the way he listened when she spoke, how he nodded at elderly women on the street and especially when he dropped a twenty-dollar bill into a little boy's saxophone case and applauded the child's feeble efforts at playing Jingle Bells. Her best friend had grown up, and the realization brought a conflicting mix of security and anxiety. He was familiar and new, all at once, and her heart had trouble determining the mixed-up pieces.

"Listen." Carter's voice lowered, and he waited until a family of four in matching T-shirts passed by before continuing. "There are probably a dozen things that still need to be said between us, and no one realizes that more than me. But why don't we just take it one day at a time? Can you do that?"

She could. But did she want to? The wind rattled some

leaves past her feet on the sidewalk, and she followed the red
and gold entanglement with her eyes. Staying bitter would
lead her nowhere. But embracing this new relationship with
Carter, whatever it might become, could help her heal—if she
could keep her heart from making the same mistake she made
seven years ago.

She made her decision. "I can try."

Immediately the answer relaxed her shoulders, and she
drew a deep breath of fresh air. The evening still stretched long
before them, and she was determined to make up for lost time.
If Carter wanted a friend, a friend he would get.

"Great." Carter stood and offered his hand to pull her up.
"Next on our tour is the Merieult House, but I am in serious
need of a hot dog from this vendor I saw earlier…"

Gracie tucked her arm through Carter's, ignoring the shiver
the contact created in her stomach. She lifted her chin. "Bet
I can eat more than you."

"You're on, shorty."

"You buying?"

"Naturally."

"Then lead the way."

"What, no argument this time?"

"Would it matter?" She laughed as he shook his head, and
they moved up toward Royal Street, admiring the holiday
decorations in storefronts and laughing at the various crawfish sporting Santa hats. One day at a time—no more dwelling on the past, no more worrying about the future. She'd offer
friendship, but not her heart.

Once was more than enough.

Chapter Seventeen

Carter drove east on I-10, away from where he'd seen Gracie home. He wasn't sure where he was going now but he needed to drive, to clear his mind. He rested his head against the seat cushion as he merged into traffic, the glow of the streetlights flashing by in a series of golden-orange blurs as he gradually increased his speed.

The evening had gone well. After the awkward talk that made him want to hide under the bench, they'd regained their footing, eaten some beignets and went over the song list as planned. The choices for the gala were now confirmed, and all he had to do was get his hands on a piano for a little while and practice. Gracie volunteered Lori's piano at their townhouse, a gesture he hoped meant that she was serious in this new friendship role he was so desperate for her to play.

Why did it matter? Why was her friendship so important to him? He couldn't let it go, let her go, again. Not after being in her warm presence, soaking up her caring personality and generous heart like a forgotten sponge.

A car horn honked and he quickly eased away from the middle line he'd been riding. He waved at the SUV with a wince. He better get his thoughts off Gracie and pay attention to his driving, or pull over. When was the last time she'd distracted him so?

Probably the night he picked her up for his senior class party. Despite the turmoil of that fateful evening, Carter couldn't help but smile at its beginning. It was the first time he'd noticed Gracie as anything more than a friend, the first time he saw the way her eyes lit when she smiled at him, the first time he admired her graceful form. Oh, he'd noticed that before, all right—he *was* a flesh and blood male and they'd gone swimming together enough times for him to notice she had grown into her long limbs. But she was still just Gracie, the girl next door who knew his secrets and was his best friend anyway.

But leaning over to pop open the passenger door of his truck that night in her driveway changed everything. She'd hauled herself into his extended cab, dressed in a green shirt that did amazing things for her eyes and her figure, and settled into the seat beside him. When their gazes met, the unspoken hello died on his lips and he could only stare—at the strands of loose hair curling around her shoulders, at the sparkly earrings grazing the softness of her neck, at the sweetness in her smile.

Carter's hands had gripped the wheel, as if afraid he might pull her into his arms. It was his mother's fault for putting those thoughts in his head. What his meddling mom didn't understand was he would never be good enough for Gracie. Gracie lived by the rules, thrived by them—he fought them at all costs. He was already not good enough for his pastoral parents. The last thing he needed was to be beaten down by an angelic girlfriend. There would be no escape then.

So he'd ignored Gracie's startling presence that night, all while bringing her fruit punch and making casual conversation and playing out his end of the bet for his friends. One hundred bucks for bringing Gracie to the party. His football buddies bet he couldn't convince the school's goody-goody to attend on his arm, but he knew otherwise. Gracie would do anything for him. Besides, he had every intention of spilling the beans afterward and sharing the spoils with her for being a good sport. But after he'd snuck a few beers and saw

Danielle Maraschino winking at him from across the room, well—the party became blurry after that.

Except for one part.

Another horn honked and Carter jerked. He flashed his blinker and pulled off the nearest exit, not realizing until he was on it that he was heading toward the church. He navigated his truck toward the parking lot at *L'Eglise de Grace* and turned off the ignition, heart still hammering in his chest. From the near wreck or the memories of his worst moment with Gracie, he wasn't sure. Shame and regret pierced his conscience, and sweat broke along his hairline.

He adjusted the visor to block the beam of the parking-lot lamp and surrendered himself to the memory of the night he lost his best friend.

She'd been sitting on the pier of his parent's property when he found her, in the same spot she'd been when he invited her to the party the week before. The impact of that wasn't lost, and suddenly, despite the foggy remainder of beer clouding his mind, it became obvious. Gracie had taken the invitation to mean much more than it did.

He'd reached in his pocket as he approached, nervously flipping his favorite guitar pick between his fingers. Gracie's shoulders shook and soft cries echoed over the still waters. Carter had perched on the edge of the pier beside her, at a loss for words. Guilt over his bad decision filled his stomach, but underneath it still remained the frustration that always came when near Gracie—born of the realization that if she weren't so perfect, maybe his parents wouldn't expect him to be.

A fact that was a joke in itself. He'd had more than his share of his father's hypocrisy from the pulpit, and as far as Carter was concerned, he couldn't escape to college fast enough. Finally finding the courage to confront his father, they'd argued in the hours before the party about the reverend's secret gambling addiction. But all Carter had gotten for his efforts was a sore jaw and stinging cheek.

One problem at a time. Carter stopped on the pier and tried to hide his frustrated sigh. "What's wrong, Blue Eyes?" He'd play it cool, let her cry and offer a hug. He knew Gracie, she wouldn't let this ruin their friendship. If anything, she'd deny the truth and blame the tears on hormones or something. He'd nod as if he understood, then go home and forget this disastrous night ever happened—and try to forget the way Gracie's smile made his stomach tingle, even while kissing Danielle.

"What's *wrong?*" Gracie turned to him with disbelief and fire highlighting the tears in her eyes. She'd swiped her cheeks with the back of her hand and shoved him so hard in the chest he almost toppled into the water. "What do you think is wrong, Carter? You used me!"

He threw out of his arms to keep his balance and edged away from her, panic gripping his insides. He wasn't prepared for this kind of anger—he'd much rather deal with tears. "Gracie, I'm sorry."

"You humiliated me." She turned to him, eyes wide with fresh tears, her slight figure illuminated by moonlight. "You set me up."

"It wasn't like that."

"Then what was it?" Her voice echoed off the water.

He shrugged, then stuffed his hands in his pockets when he realized they were shaking. "I thought we'd split the money, and laugh about it later." The honest explanation suddenly sounded weak. He swallowed the regret rising in his throat.

"That's pathetic." She turned away, disgust written on her face.

"Maybe, but it's true." Carter risked a step closer to her, the wooden piers creaking under his feet. "I wouldn't hurt you on purpose. You know that."

"I don't know what I know anymore." She sniffed, one hand reaching up to wipe at her eyes.

"Gracie, you know *me*. Come on."

The crickets seemed impossibly loud in her pointed silence.

He dragged his hand through his hair. "I'm sorry, okay? I'm sorry. With cherries or whatever else you want to put on top." He thought the joke of Gracie's commonly used expression would make her smile, but her face remained like stone.

"That's not good enough this time."

"You've forgiven me for worse. What about the time I got gum in your hair and you had to cut it shoulder length in middle school?"

"That was different."

"What's different about it? I hurt you both times, and neither was intentional. Do you not believe that?"

She raised her eyes to him then, and he stepped back at the vulnerability in her expression. "I'm different."

"I'm not following, Gracie." Man, he shouldn't have drunk that last beer. He shouldn't have even brought Gracie to the party in the first place. Maybe his friends were right. Maybe she was too good for his crowd. Why'd he have to go and try to prove otherwise? For a little cash and the sake of a laugh with his buddies, he'd hurt his best friend.

The moon highlighted the bronze in Gracie's hair as she flipped it over her shoulders in the familiar way she always did when she was nervous—and in that moment, he knew. They weren't best friends anymore.

"You really don't see it, do you?"

"See what?" He averted his eyes away from her searching gaze, wanting to deny the inevitable for as long as he could—for one more song, for one more chorus from the cricket choir, for one more round of the wave's melody against the aging dock. His heart sank like the pebbles he and Gracie used to skip on this very water.

Gracie shook her head with a hoarse laugh. "You know what I'm talking about. Don't be stupid." She shoved him again, but this time he grabbed her arms and held on tight.

"Tell me."

She struggled in his grip as fresh tears fell. "You know how I feel about you! How I've always felt."

His hold loosened and shock reeled his senses. "Always felt?"

She wrenched her arms free and rubbed them with both hands. "You've had my heart since we were little kids, Carter. It took me a while to see it but once I did, I couldn't see anything else." She sniffed. "Despite knowing better, I love you."

The pier seemed to spin. Carter swallowed hard, disbelief numbing his reactions. "Love me?" He shoved his hands in his pockets, backing away from her. "No, you don't. I'm your friend, Gracie. You're confused." His heart stammered double time in his chest and he wanted to scream. *No, no, no!* Not this, not now. Not after the fight with his dad. Too much was changing at once. He clamped his hands into fists.

"I've never been more sure of anything." She stepped toward him, one hand reaching out as if she hadn't moments ago been wrestling away. "I love you, Carter, as more than a friend—much more."

"No!" He hadn't meant to yell, but the sharp word broke the rhythmic sounds of the waves lapping against the pier and the frogs whistling from the upper branches of the Cypress trees. "No, you don't. I won't let you."

"You don't have a choice." Gracie's hand fell to her side and hung limply by her dirt-smudged black pants. Her voice lowered and she stared at her feet. "Neither do I."

He took another step back, wishing this night had never happened. Then nothing would have changed—her feelings would have remained a secret and he wouldn't be sporting fresh bruises from his father. "You have to stop."

"I can't." Her barely audible words pierced his heart, and gut-wrenching agony seeped into his stomach.

"Gracie, I'm leaving."

"What?" Her head snapped up.

The spontaneous words made a lot of sense. He wasn't supposed to head for college until the end of July, but sticking around seemed unbearable. He was sick of sitting in church and pretending he didn't know his father was pretending, sick of being stifled from what he was—a musician, a free spirit. No one understood him—and the one person he thought did suddenly understood something he couldn't. "I'm leaving. In two weeks."

The idea settled like a balm to his churning stomach. Two weeks. That was plenty of time to pack up after the graduation ceremony and head for LSU early, maybe make a few road trip stops along the way. The glimpse of freedom strengthened his resolve. "I don't know what you expect from me, Gracie, but I don't see you that way. Never will." The lie burned his lips, and he hated the way she winced as if slapped.

"I see." Her words parted the grief in his heart and he almost withdrew his statement. But he couldn't take it back now, couldn't face his father and couldn't tell anyone, much less Gracie, the truth about her pastor.

He squared his shoulders. "I hope so." He clasped his guitar pick for courage and tossed his hair out of his eyes. "I'll see ya around, Blue Eyes." He turned and began to walk down the pier toward land.

"Just like that, huh?" Gracie's hurt tone carried down the length of the wooden beams and assaulted his back. "Everything we've gone through together—that's it?"

Tears spiked her words, but Carter kept walking, back straight, head forward. From this angle, she wouldn't be able to see the tears in his own eyes. "Just like that."

"I should have known, Carter Alexander." Her voice cracked but he kept walking, legs unsteady, wishing he could plug his ears against her desperate, verbal assault. "I should have known you weren't any different. Enjoy your cash—hope it was worth it."

He drew a deep breath and fired one last, quiet shot over his shoulder. "I didn't take the money."

Chapter Eighteen

Sitting in his truck at the church parking lot, a tear slipped unbidden from Carter's eye at the memory of that long ago night. He quickly wiped away the evidence of his lifelong regret.

Lord, when did I become such an idiot? Carter rested his forehead against the cool leather steering wheel and considered banging his head against it, though the act would only give him a bruise rather than much-needed clarity.

After spending the afternoon with Gracie, he knew he couldn't just be her friend. He was a fool to think he could spin back the hands of time and not want to seize the chance to be to Gracie what she'd wanted—needed—all those years ago. But if they were having this much trouble redefining their friendship now, how could he ever expect her to trust him with her heart again? *Fool me once, shame on you, fool me twice…* The old adage ran like a sad record through his mind, and he groaned.

It was impossible. He could never explain to Gracie his motivation for leaving her that night, could never share the details of his teenage emotional blow-up without revealing his father's secret. The reverend might lie in a grave, but Carter refused to dishonor him by airing his laundry—it would only prove his dad's point of how Carter never could do the right thing. Yet without that explanation, Gracie would never open up. Not like she used to.

Somewhere outside the silence of his truck, a dog barked. Horns honked and the bass of a nearby car radio thumped a beat as it passed on the road. All around him was proof of life. Everyone else managed to go about their daily tasks without being locked in the prison of the past.

Carter rubbed his hands over his face, wishing he could rub power back into his tired, emotionally weary brain. He glanced up and with a rush of relief, noticed Andy's car was parked under the covered drop-off area in front of the auditorium. He should go inside, see what Andy was up to—maybe they could play a quick game of one-on-one in the gym and burn off these memories. Though if Carter were smart, he'd head back to Andy's apartment and practice the songs he would be performing at the gala. The sooner they got this whole ordeal over with, the better—for Gracie's sake and his own.

But his legs felt molded to the floor of the cab, clutched in an invisible vice that refused to let go. Something lingered in his conscience, hovering on the edge of his memory and refusing to loosen its grip until acknowledged. But what?

I don't have a choice. Like the wind across the lake, Gracie's words from nearly a decade ago whispered through his mind, carrying the same anguish with which they were spoken that night. She admitted she didn't have a choice in loving him, that he couldn't stop her and implying that she couldn't stop herself.

Carter's heartbeat accelerated, and his palms grew slick against the steering wheel as hope dared to strum a chord of possibility. Had that truth changed? If the miserable look in her eyes that night on the pier meant anything, than Gracie had no more control over her feelings now than she did back then. Love didn't disintegrate over seven years. It could be repressed, maybe, hidden beneath layers of regret, but not eliminated—not true love.

He knew his feelings for Gracie hadn't tempered in the

least. They'd been denied, ignored, cast aside, but never disposed of—even after all they'd been through.

Was there hope she felt the same?

Carter pulled his keys from the ignition and opened the door of the truck. His feet hit the concrete with a light step and he pocketed the keys with a smile he couldn't contain. He strode toward the gymnasium doors, his shoulders finally seeming free of burden for the first time since laying eyes on Gracie behind the glass exhibit. Sure, he needed a second opinion, needed to pray about this new twist of thought. It was a long shot, but maybe, just maybe there was a chance for them to return to love after all.

Gracie teasingly blasted Huey with a gush of water from the hose. He brayed in indignation and belly flopped into his pool, as if to prove he wanted to get wet anyway. With a laugh, Gracie turned her attention back to the deck she was cleaning and bent to scrub a particularly stained spot with a brush. Water seeped through the knees of her khaki pants, and she rubbed her forehead with the back of one damp hand. At least it was almost closing time, and no one would see her disheveled appearance except the birds, and they were used to it.

Gumbo waddled past, as if to investigate her chore. "I'm cleaning up after you. Want to help?" Gracie held out her brush, and Gumbo fluttered his wings. "Guess that's a no." She stuck out her tongue and resumed scrubbing. After the exhibit was clean, she could change into the extra clothes she'd brought and try to catch the end of the Cajun dinner fundraiser going on at the church.

It was only two weeks before the big gala event. Andy had suggested she keep thinking of fund-raiser ideas, just in the case the fund-raisers as a whole didn't bring in enough money, but so far, her mind was a blank. Well, not a complete blank. It was full of items from her to-do list, details about the daily care of her penguins and concern over whether the gala would be a success. Mostly she stayed occupied with trying to keep Carter *out* of her mind—a task that was proving to be impossible, especially after their walking-tour date the afternoon before.

A knock against the display startled Gracie from her thoughts, and she sat upright with a surprised blink. Carter waved at her through the glass from the hallway. Gracie hesitated, then waved back, holding up one finger to indicate she'd be out in a minute. She peeled off her gloves and pushed up the water-spotted sleeves of her polo. How many times had he seen her in this dirty uniform now? Three? She told herself it didn't matter, then gathered her cleaning supplies and stowed them in the supply room outside the exhibit. She locked the door, then took the stairs down into the hallway, trying to ignore her rushing heart. Why was he here?

"Hey." Carter's smile increased her erratic pulse and she brushed back her hair with a damp hand.

"Hi. Everything okay at the church? I thought you'd be up to your elbows in spices by now."

"Andy's manning the grill, and the kids found him a chef's hat." Carter laughed. "Everything is surprisingly under control. I came to see if you wanted a ride out there."

"You did?" Gracie's lips parted, and she quickly brought them back together. She'd spent the majority of her Saturday afternoon trying not to picture the way Carter and Tawny were surely working together—Tawny's high-pitched laugh, her not-so-subtle suggestions, her revealing wardrobe...

"I missed— I mean, the kids missed you. Haley's been asking me every five minutes if you were coming, so..." His voice trailed off and he shrugged with a small smile. "Maybe they'll like me more if I bring you to them."

"They like you just fine on their own. But I'd appreciate a ride. Let me change real quick—I doubt anyone wants to smell *au de penguin* at a cookout." Her face flushed, and she told herself it was just from knowing the kids wanted her around. Had Haley really said that, or was Carter covering for his verbal blunder?

"No problem. I'll wait for you right outside the front doors." Carter gestured with his head in the general direction of the lobby.

"Be right back." Gracie turned toward her office to grab her stowed duffel bag, her mind racing faster than Huey after a fresh fish. Regardless of the kids influence, Carter had taken the time to come all the way to her work to offer her a ride. The fact that he left Tawny had to mean something, right?

But just yesterday she'd become set on friendship, nothing more. Why couldn't her heart keep up with her head? Gracie shouldered the wide strap of her duffel bag and locked her office door before heading toward the restrooms to change. She needed to get a firm grip on her emotions, before she went back to acting like a high schooler and overanalyzing Carter's every move. That's what got her in trouble last time, thinking he invited her to that party as something more than a friend. She should have known better then—and wasn't about to fall for it now and have to give herself the same lecture twice.

"I'm so full." Carter pressed a hand against his stomach and groaned.

Gracie smirked and reached farther across the cardboard table with her wet rag to wipe down the other side. "Then why'd you eat two burgers and a bowl of gumbo?"

"You must not have seen that plateful of bread pudding." Lori twisted the cap on the almost empty bottle of soda and set it in a plastic bag with the other leftover drinks.

"It was a desert plate," Carter protested. "Shouldn't have held so much." He slipped lower in the folding chair.

"It was worth it. Carter's share of food alone was enough for the new penguin exhibit." Lori held up the bank bag, stuffed full of cash from the fund-raiser.

"Hardly." Gracie laughed. "Though it does seem we were successful today." The long hours had been rough on everyone, but the kids appeared happy to have helped and went home with free leftovers. Andy, Lori and Gracie decided to clean up and let them leave early, after having worked so hard. Carter had also volunteered to help put away supplies, but at the moment, seemed content to wallow in his chair and complain.

Gracie still wasn't sure how such a whiny man could seem so attractive.

"Better have been, after all that smoke I inhaled." Andy shoved two more folding chairs onto the roll-away cart and grinned. "I smell like a turkey."

"Did we even have turkey?" Gracie stopped wiping and frowned.

"Boudin. It sold out before you and Carter got back from the aquarium," Lori answered.

"Hey, where did Tawny go?" Andy stacked another chair and then looked around the deserted gym. "She said she'd take the leftover pasta salad home."

"She left about thirty minutes ago." Lori handed Gracie the bag of cash and began gathering up the remaining paper plates from the second table. "Said something about not feeling well."

"I hope it wasn't the boudin." Andy frowned.

Gracie worked to keep her face neutral. It wasn't the pork and turkey mix stuffed in sausage that had made Tawny leave, it was that Carter had made every effort possible to ignore her. The fact hadn't gone lost on the girl, nor on Gracie. *What is he up to?* It was nice having the old Carter back for a few hours, joking around and spreading his charm equally throughout the group instead of on the prettiest woman in the room. But she wouldn't be tricked that easily. One night did not equal a life change.

"I doubt she even had any. I'll check on her tomorrow if she's not at church." Gracie ducked her head as she pretended to study the contents of the bank bag, letting her hair curtain her face. Hopefully Andy wouldn't see the telltale burn she felt creeping up her neck.

"Thanks, Gracie. All right, looks like we're about done here." Andy surveyed the gym with his fingers hooked through the belt loops of his jeans. "Carter, man, you need a wheelbarrow, or can you drive home?"

"I prefer to roll." Carter groaned. He stood, and Andy scooped up the last folding chair he'd been sitting on and added it to the cart.

"You know what sounds good?" Lori's eyes narrowed as she stared toward the gym door. "A beignet."

"Are you kidding me?" Carter pretended to stagger to one side.

Lori laughed. "Some of us didn't eat one of everything. Gracie, you want to come with me?"

Gracie started to agree, but Carter held up one hand. "Actually, I was about to ask if you girls would let me use the piano in your townhouse. I need to practice for the gala, since that's the instrument I'll be using the most during the show. I was going to use the church piano, but I found out tonight it's broken."

"Repairman coming next week." Andy shook his head. "Don't even ask. Let's just say it involves our new church pianist and a few hairpins too many."

"Is it okay with you, Gracie?"

Carter's eyes met hers and she found herself agreeing before she could decide if it bothered her or not. He was doing her a favor for the gala, how could she refuse him what he needed in order to practice? But her heart hung heavy as a dumbbell in her chest.

Lori pushed open the double gym doors. "Great. You go home and let him in, and I'll grab some beignets to go and meet you guys back at the house. Andy, you want in on this?"

"No, thanks." Andy pulled the church keys from his pocket and plucked out the one for the gym door. "I'll lock up after you guys, then I'm going home to crash. Those kids wore me out tonight. I thought youth ministers received extra energy when they were ordained." He rubbed his eyes with the back of his hand.

"Nah, just extra patience." Lori winked and pushed open the double doors of the gym. "Gracie, see you and Carter in a few."

Gracie waved to her friend, then followed Carter outside to his truck, nodding as he mentioned something about swinging by the aquarium to pick up her car. Maybe she should get in her own vehicle and just drive away. Claim a flat tire later, anything to delay seeing Carter cozying up to their piano, invading her personal space. So much for her plans of a bubble bath and a good book at home.

Her evening would be spent protecting her heart.

Chapter Nineteen

"Want anything to drink?" Gracie sank down onto the sofa, tucking her sock-clad feet underneath her.

"No thanks." Carter shifted on the bench of the piano, edging back so his feet were the right distance from the pedals. His fingers trailed over the ivory keys. A chill grazed his skin and he shivered. How many of these had he played over the years? Dozens, if not more. Grands, baby grands, uprights—some touched before by people far more famous than himself. But this piano, though new to his touch, stirred up memories he couldn't forget—melodies hummed with Gracie's mezzo-soprano singing softly along. He could still hear their voices blending together, could hear echoes of past numbers performed by him and Gracie for their family and friends. They could have been a hit together.

Maybe they still could.

He swallowed the emotion burning the back of his throat. "Do you remember the first time I tried to teach you how to play the piano?"

Gracie snorted. "Tried is right."

"You weren't that bad."

"Your brain must have blocked it out." Gracie rolled her eyes. "The neighbor's cat started howling. It was more a lesson of what keys *not* to hit."

"I don't believe you."

"You were there!"

"You're exaggerating." He grinned. Man, he missed teasing her.

"Do you really not remember? Trust me when I say it was painful for all involved. Your mother had to wear earplugs."

Carter patted the piano bench next to him. "Prove it."

Gracie sucked in her breath. Carter held his. Would she trust him, or would it be another show of two steps forward, three steps back?

Slowly, Gracie stood and approached the bench. Carter's heart raced at the small victory, and he slid over to give her room. She sank onto the wooden seat and flexed her fingers over the keys.

"It's been a while."

"It's okay. There you go. Where's C?" Carter fought the urge to place his hand over hers and guide. He released a deep breath. *One step at a time.*

She pressed the correct key and the chord sounded across the living room.

"Good. What about F?"

"You must be kidding." Gracie laughed, but her shoulders were so tense her entire back resembled a straight line.

Carter showed her the F key. "You must have been playing by ear that day." The details of the lesson with Gracie when they were teens blurred into an indescribable mass of off-key notes and giggles. He could hear her laughter, feel the grin he wore as Gracie tried and failed to mimic his music, remembered the camaraderie and inside jokes.

But the one part that remained all too vivid was the wink and knowing smile his mother offered as she poked her head around the doorframe from the kitchen. The lesson ended not five minutes later, and Carter sought refuge from the frustration with his guitar and a six-pack.

His mouth went dry. What would have happened that day if he had stayed and let Gracie play longer? Yet another question to remain forever unanswered.

Gracie stirred on the bench beside him. "I think you're right about playing by ear. That's what I did as a teenager."

"Try it again. Pick a hymn, something familiar, and give it a shot."

Gracie frowned, but reached for the keys. Doubt prickled her forehead and Carter squeezed his hands together to keep from smoothing the wrinkle in her skin. She began to play, haltingly.

"Good."

"Liar." She laughed and her shoulders seemed to loosen with the movement.

"Keep going." He scooted an eighth of an inch closer. The floral scent of her shampoo teased his senses and he inhaled deeply. She used to smell like vanilla. What other subtle changes had Gracie made in her life since he'd been absent? He wanted to know them all.

She pressed a few more keys. Carter began to make out the strains of "Amazing Grace." "Nice."

"Really?" She kept her eyes on the keyboard, stumbling over the next note before finding the correct one. A small smile lit the corners of her mouth.

"Really." Carter leaned in, taking advantage of the opportunity to study Gracie's profile undetected—the tiny dimple by her mouth, the furrow of her brow as she concentrated.

She continued to play, the notes gaining strength as her confidence increased. Carter moved in closer, knowing he was crowding her space but unable to keep his distance. He wanted to be close, wanted to feel the music she played, wanted to pretend like the last several years hadn't happened and that all was right in the world—and they were together.

"Gracie, I—" Her name fell off his lips before he could catch himself, and she jerked, her fingers hovering over the keys.

"What'd I do? Did I hit the wrong note?" She looked up, concern lighting her eyes.

"No. You did nothing wrong." Carter covered one of her hands with his. Her entire body stiffened with the contact. "I did."

"Carter, what are you talking about?" Gracie pulled free from his touch, her heart feeling as if it might burst from her chest and bounce across the piano keys. She folded her hands in her lap, back stiff, afraid to move—afraid not to move.

"I'm not sure if I can do this, Gracie." Carter touched the end of her sleeve where it met her wrist and she shivered.

He was too close. She had to get away, back to a safe distance. She stood, eager for escape. "Do what?" But she knew. She felt it, too, the chemistry pulsing through the room like a separate heartbeat.

Carter caught her hand, and despite knowing better, Gracie looked down at him on the bench and their gazes held.

Gracie yanked her arm free. "Carter, you can't— You said you wouldn't—" Words slipped her mind and she struggled for a coherent thought. "Friends." That's all she could say, the only word that made sense. She repeated it in a desperate attempt for survival. "Friends."

In one quick movement, Carter leaped from the bench, knocking the wooden seat over, and moved in front of her. His arms rested on the sides of the piano, trapping her in his loose embrace. "Are we, Gracie? Is that all we are?"

Her breath caught and her eyes searched his, desperate for clarity. Why couldn't he leave things alone? She opened her mouth, then closed it, afraid of what to say yet more afraid to keep quiet.

He ducked his head, then raised his eyes to meet hers, a lock of dark hair falling across his forehead. "I want to kiss you."

Gracie's eyes widened. The room tilted under her feet. "Carter, I—"

Carter leaned forward, his breath warm against her cheek, arms still braced on her either side. "Say the word, and I'll move. But if you don't, then I'm going to kiss you."

She swallowed the lump in her throat and commanded her legs to move, to carry her sideways, to put pressure against his arms and let him know she wanted out. But her traitorous legs refused to obey, and she remained fixed in one spot, heart racing as if she'd just run a marathon.

Carter's gaze searched hers for permission, and despite the anxiety knotting in her stomach, she knew her eyes gave just that.

He closed the distance between them quickly, as if she might change her mind, and brushed his lips against hers. Her mind flipped in sync with her stomach, and she shut her eyes, feeling as if she were eighteen once again and finally getting her most secret wish.

He pulled away an inch, then kissed her again. She returned the kiss, the years of regret and anger and betrayal melted away into his heartfelt apology. Time seemed to rewind, flashing frames of memories like windows on a train.

The front door opened, and footsteps sounded on the tile entryway, followed by a loud rustle. Carter pulled away. Disoriented, as if waking from a dream, Gracie peered over his broad shoulders. Lori stood by the door, her mouth open and a white sack of pastries in her hand. Gracie gasped.

Lori's gape turned into a smirk as realization crossed her pleased expression. "Hope I didn't interrupt anything."

Chapter Twenty

❧

"This is a disaster." Andy's hands landed on the top of his desk with a thud. "Half the people we served food to yesterday are sick."

"Sick?" Gracie tucked her Bible under her arm and frowned. "What do you mean?"

"Sick, as in, stuck in the restroom for hours. Which is where Carter camped out all night and why he missed church this morning."

"I wondered where he was." She'd had a hard time concentrating on the sermon, due to the variety of doubts assaulting her mind and wondering if their kiss had anything to do with his absence. The tension in her shoulders eased. She hated that Carter didn't feel well, but at least she knew he wasn't avoiding her.

Andy rolled backward in his office chair and crossed his hands over his stomach. "He's miserable. I don't see how I avoided it—I guess I didn't eat as much as he did."

"You think it was food poisoning?"

"I don't know what to think. I just know that almost forty people have left voicemails this morning asking for refunds—some not so politely."

"Refunds?" Gracie sagged against the doorframe. "But we can't—"

"We might not have a choice. I can't let the church get a bad reputation from this. We should take responsibility for whatever happened. I just don't understand..." Andy's voice trailed off as he rubbed his temples with his fingers. "I've cooked for groups a dozen times before. Everything was fresh."

Panic seized Gracie's insides. Refunds meant zero profit— in fact, it might even mean she owed the church since they covered the upfront cost of the food. Without any sales, they'd be in the hole that amount of money. It was only fair. She squeezed her eyes shut and did some quick calculations. If she paid the church back with the profits from the other fund-raising events... She finished the rough tally and the resulting number made her groan.

"I better go check on the kids. I left them in the gym with Tawny and Lori." Andy stood and scooted his chair under his desk. "If you want to call and check on Carter, tell him I'm praying for him."

"I will." Gracie stayed in the doorframe of Andy's office as he slipped by, offering her a consoling pat on the shoulder.

"Don't worry, it's just one fund-raiser. We made money off the rest and the aquarium discount tickets should still bring in what you need."

"I just hate to think of that wasted food and effort. Not to mention all those sick people."

Andy shrugged. "It's just one of those things. Did you eat anything that day?"

Gracie frowned, trying to remember. "No, I got there late and was so busy, I don't think I ate anything except a few of the cookies someone brought."

"Good thing." Andy smiled, but it looked tense around the edges. "Maybe you can help me distribute the refunds this week."

"Of course." She'd make time for that somehow, around all the other last-minute gala work that had to be done. She and Lori still hadn't nailed down the final decorations, not to mention all the phone calls that needed to be made, and the signs that still needed posting.

She watched as Andy hurried toward the gym. It was Sunday morning—less than two weeks until the big event, and at this rate, the gala was going to be nothing but an empty room in the hotel banquet hall at the *Château de Sommeil* and bunch of fancy food from a caterer she couldn't afford.

The doors at the other end of the hall opened. Tawny tossed her brown hair over her shoulders as she approached Gracie. "Have you seen Andy? The kids started throwing paper airplanes and Lori can't get them to quit."

"He was just heading your way." Gracie tried to smile. "Are you feeling all right? Apparently everyone who ate at the cookout yesterday is pretty sick."

A smile teased the edges of Tawny's mouth, then disappeared so fast Gracie wondered if she even saw it. "That's too bad. I feel fine. But I didn't eat much." She patted her slim waist. "You know how it is…well, maybe not." She smirked.

Gracie swallowed the retort rising in her throat. "Glad you're okay. Carter is sick at home, too, according to Andy."

"Poor thing." But the expression that crossed Tawny's face was one of disdain, not sympathy. "I better get back to the gym. See ya." She flounced back down the hall with a final toss of her wavy hair.

Gracie watched her go. Something wasn't right with Tawny. She was even more aloof than usual. Jealous? But why—there was no way she could know that Carter had kissed her.

As if by their own will, her fingers reached up and touched her lips. After Lori interrupted last night, the moment vanished and the three of them had spent the next hour munching beignets and rehearsing at the piano—all while ignoring the giant elephant that had taken up residence in the corner of the living room.

She and Carter needed to talk—soon. They couldn't pretend nothing had happened, not with a history like theirs. Did the kiss change anything? Was it a symbol of commitment on Carter's part, or a onetime expression of emotion? A culmination of feelings, or an offer of something permanent?

There she went, overanalyzing again. Gracie tightened her grip on the Bible in her hands and lifted her chin. She would take it one day at a time, like they already discussed. Just because they kissed didn't mean anything had changed. And just because it was everything she ever hoped it would be didn't mean the betrayal of the past was forgotten.

Carter never wanted to see a hamburger again. Or bread pudding. He groaned at the memory and sipped from his glass of ginger ale. Saltines would suffice for the immediate future. The half-empty stick of crackers seemed to mock him from the coffee table. Boring, but safe—he'd take it.

From his viewpoint in the recliner, he could just see the kitchen clock. Twelve-thirty. Church was out—Andy would be back soon, no doubt to tease him more. That's what he got for overeating, he supposed, but man, last night had been brutal.

The doorbell rang. Carter groaned. Now he had to get up. He wiped cracker crumbs off the legs of his lounge pants and stood from the recliner, wobbling slightly. He was probably nearing dehydration. He stumbled to the door. If this was Andy making him get up as a joke when he had his key the whole time...

Gracie smiled when he yanked open the door. "Feeling better?"

"Gracie, hey, I'm— What are you—" Carter made a feeble attempt to smooth his hair. Not exactly the way he wanted their first meeting to go after last night's kiss—and of course he hadn't showered yet. He edged back a step.

Gracie must have taken that as a sign to come in. "Andy said you were sick last night. He's staying at the church with the youth for a while, so I thought I'd check on you." She twisted her fingers around her purse strap in a nervous gesture. So the kiss had shaken her up.

That made two of them.

He shut the door and motioned her toward the couch. "I think the worst is over. I'm not sure what happened."

Gracie sat on the sofa, smoothing her black skirt over her knees. "I do. Andy said almost everyone who ate at the cook-out yesterday is sick."

"How does he know?" Carter eased back into the recliner.

She sighed. "Because they've all called, wanting refunds."

"Oh, no. But the gala…"

"Exactly."

"I'm so sorry, Gracie. What rotten timing to stumble across some bad meat." Carter shook his head.

"I'm not convinced that's all it was." Gracie crossed her ankles, staring down at her lap. "I'm pretty sure someone did it on purpose."

Carter snorted. "Who would want to sabotage a church fund-raiser?" He knew Gracie was disappointed about losing the money, but this idea was reaching. If she was that desperate, maybe he could help her out. He could donate a little cash toward the gala to make up the difference in what they lost. He could spare it for now—if she'd take it.

Gracie bit her lower lip. "Tawny."

"Tawny?" Carter's eyebrows rose, his idea to help momentarily forgotten as surprise rocked his senses. "Are you serious? She wasn't even there for very long."

"I know. She left early, but Lori said she was helping Andy cook."

"For a little while, yes, but that doesn't mean she poisoned the food." Carter rubbed his forehead. Was Gracie so insecure about his feelings for her that she had resorted to random accusations? Had the kiss last night meant nothing to her—or for that matter, all the hints he'd dropped over the last week?

Women. And all this on an empty stomach.

"I don't know for sure." Gracie's voice raised an octave. "But she was acting very strange at the church today and didn't seem all that bothered, or surprised for that matter, about you or anyone else being sick."

"So that makes her guilty?"

Gracie's face hardened. "Why are you so determined to defend her?"

"You didn't answer my question."

"You didn't answer mine."

They stared at each other.

Carter blew out a slow breath. "Look, Gracie—"

"Forget it." She stood up, back rigid. "I'll talk to you later." She started for the door.

"I wasn't defending—"

"Yes, you were." She spun around, her skirt swirling around her legs. "Look, I've been nothing but nice to Tawny since the day she first showed up at the church. Even after…" Her voice trailed off and she looked away, a tinge of red creeping up her neck.

"After what?" Carter stepped toward her but the look in Gracie's eyes when she met his stopped him cold.

"Even after she made a play for you."

"She didn't—" He couldn't finish the sentence honestly. Tawny *had* come on to him, he just hadn't realized it as quickly as Gracie and Andy. But why the drama if he'd turned Tawny down? This didn't make any sense.

"Have you ever known me to accuse someone unjustly? I'm not trying to start rumors, Carter, I'm trying to get to the bottom of whatever is going on and whoever is costing the church their hard-earned money. I had a hunch and thought I could talk about it with you." She took another step toward the door. "Guess you're still too blinded to see the truth—as usual."

"What do you mean by that?" All compassion fled as her words slapped him across the heart.

"You're a sucker for a pretty face! If I was trying to talk about a man in the church wrecking the gala you'd be all for the discussion."

"That's not fair—"

"It never is, is it?" Gracie shook her hair out of her eyes. "What about kissing me last night, after all that talk you gave me about us just being friends? How was that fair?"

rter clenched his fists at his sides. First she was upset se he defended Tawny, now she was upset because he'd shown Gracie his feelings for *her?* She was completely contradicting herself. "I didn't force that kiss on you."

"No, you didn't." She briefly pressed her lips together. "But I should have known better than to open myself up. Nothing has changed."

"Gracie, *everything* has changed. I'm not the same guy you used to know. I thought I'd proven that time and time again." He felt like banging his head against the front door. Maybe his medicine was making him hallucinate—surely this frustrating conversation wasn't actually happening. Would his mistakes from the past always appear in random moments to rub in his face? Times like these reminded him of why he never wanted to be with Gracie in the first place. She was too pure, too wholesome, too perfect.

Too good for him.

Gracie's gaze pierced his, her eyes shiny with tears. "Why can't you just be more like your father?"

Her words—so spontaneous but with the edge of a knife—sliced through any remaining shards of Carter's patience. He rocked back on his heels, reeling from the unexpected wound. "More like my father?" The harsh laugh that erupted from his mouth knocked Gracie back a step. "So you'd prefer me to be hypocritical?" He was treading on dangerous ground but he couldn't stop the words that poured from his lips—a confession almost a decade in the making. "You'd prefer me to stand behind a pulpit and preach God's word while spending the church's money at the casino boats and giving my son black eyes at home? Is that what you want?"

Her blue eyes widened and her lips parted. "What are you talking about?"

"Welcome to the truth, Gracie." He wanted to take it back, yet at the same time, he wanted to tell her everything. His stomach twisted with the rash decision but it was too late now. The words were there, hanging between them, begging to be resolved.

Her stunned expression slowly dissolved into a hard shell. "You're lying."

Carter blinked. Of all the responses he'd expected, that was the last.

"You're just saying that because you know how close your father and I were. You were always jealous of our friendship."

"That's not true." He winced. "Okay, so I probably felt like that at times. But I'm not making this up. There was a side to my dad you know nothing about. Why do you think he made all those contributions to the aquarium in the first place? And the children's hospitals? And the museums?"

"He was a good man." Her chin lifted slightly.

"Fine, Gracie. Keep him on that pedestal. If you want to be naive, go right ahead." He leaned against the wall with a sigh. So much for a confession. Gracie still refused to think badly of his father—and why not, when she could lay all her frustration on his shoulders?

"You're being ridiculous. Reverend Alexander wanted the best for you, he told me that all the time." She wiped tears from the corners of her eyes. "You were too busy with your guitars and women to ever notice."

"Is that what you think?"

"The truth hurts, doesn't it?" Her arms crossed protectively over her middle and she set her jaw in that stubborn way she always had.

"Not if you refuse to see it." Carter reached past her and opened the front door. She needed to leave, now. Before he said something he couldn't take back. All they'd been through, and she thought he'd resorted to lying to her face? That stung worse than the scorpion bite he'd gotten in eighth grade. Gracie had ridden with him and his parents to the E.R. as his ankle swelled bigger and bigger. He thought nothing could ever hurt worse.

Until now.

Gracie stepped through the doorframe and turned, her purse clutched against her chest, her eyes two blazing weapons. "Oh, I see plenty, Carter. Trust me."

He stared after her as she marched to her car, her words ringing in his ears with all the finality of a song's closing chord.

Chapter Twenty-One

Tuesday morning, Gracie sat at the desk in her office at the aquarium, staring at the phone. She should call Carter. Should just pick up the phone, dial Andy's home number, and tell Carter thanks, but no thanks. She didn't need him for the gala. She needed a musician, yes—but not him. She couldn't imagine actually letting Carter sing at her event as if nothing had happened, as if he hadn't scarred her heart all over again.

And how dare he say those things about his father? Even two days later, indignation burned in her gut. Did Carter think that trying to shift the blame to his dad and off himself would actually work? She snorted. Unlikely. Reverend Alexander was as close to perfect as she'd ever come across—one would have to be in order to put up with a past like Carter's.

"Do it. Just pick it up and dial." Gracie stared at the receiver. Maybe if she looked hard enough, the courage she needed would appear and she could get it over with. Then she could start fresh, Carter-free for the second time in her life, and call her list of musicians again. Surely someone was available by now—cancellations happened all the time, right? Her hopes lifted slightly as she focused on the phone. It wasn't that hard. Just reach forward and dial—

The phone jangled in its base. Gracie jumped, one leg kicking out and banging into the underside of the desk. She pressed her hand over the throbbing joint and grabbed the phone with the other. "Aquarium of the Americas, this is Gracie." She winced at her breathless tone. Wow, that *hurt*— and somehow, she knew it was Carter's fault, too.

"Ms. Broussard, this is Jenson Pierce with the Louisiana Aquarium. We spoke a few weeks ago about the fund-raiser you're conducting for our displaced penguins?"

Gracie leaned forward, the pain in her knee all but forgotten. "Yes, Mr. Pierce, hello. We've actually made great progress in our plans. I'm hoping for a successful event." *That is, if the caterer doesn't mind being paid in Monopoly money, and I can find another musician who can do more than hum a few bars of "Jolly Old St. Nick"....*

"That's wonderful." Relief filled the older man's voice. "I've been the penguin keeper here for over a decade, and these little guys— Well, you understand."

Gracie glanced at the framed photo of the birds on her desk. Her heart sank as doubts plagued her senses. "Yes, sir, I believe I do." Could she really cancel Carter's performance? As much as she hated to admit it, his name would draw a bigger crowd—and bigger crowds meant more donations toward the exhibit. She squeezed her eyes shut briefly.

"I just wanted to call and tell you thanks again for being so accommodating. If there's anything I can do from this end, please let me know. I'm so relieved that these birds of mine will be going to a safe place." Mr. Pierce chuckled. "Not to mention an aquarium within driving distance."

"You'll be welcome here anytime." Gracie forced a smile. "We're happy to help. I just hope we can raise the money we need."

"I have no doubt you will." Mr. Pierce's tone softened. "Keep in touch, Ms. Broussard."

"Please, call me Gracie."

"Gracie, I appreciate this more than you know. I'll say an extra prayer for your gala's success."

The phone clicked. Gracie set the receiver back in its cradle with a shaky hand. Now what? The penguin keeper at the closing aquarium called to tell her he would pray for their success, literally seconds before she cancelled their only musician for the gala? Coincidence didn't seem an appropriate description.

Gracie sighed, fighting what she knew to be true. There'd be no calling Carter today. She tapped her fingernail against the base of the phone. Maybe this could still work. Carter already had the approved song list, so she didn't have to deal with him any more before the gala. She could stay out of the house while he practiced on their piano.

Surely he wouldn't show up at the aquarium fund-raiser this Friday for the penguin IMAX movie. In fact, if he had any sense at all, he wouldn't see her until the night of the big event—during which she'd be so busy, she could easily avoid him. Besides, he'd be on stage most of the night.

Decision made, Gracie turned back to her spreadsheet. She'd filled in the blanks in the budget with the money they'd earned so far through the fund-raisers, but she hadn't deducted the amount she owed the church from the loss of profit. The image of Tawny's smirk Sunday filled Gracie's mind and her eyes narrowed. She still wasn't convinced of the woman's innocence, but she also still couldn't prove otherwise.

With a sigh, she squinted at the numbers on the screen. Might as well forget her theory about Tawny now—if no one was going to believe Gracie, it didn't matter. She'd just have to wait…and pray.

"A little bit to the right. No, your other right."

Gracie stretched the corner of the red banner she held farther in the opposite direction, her arm aching almost as much as her back. The sun beat down on the top of her hair, warming her head despite the cool wind biting through the long sleeves of her polo. Lori was having way too much fun with her instructions. And why wouldn't she? She was on the ground, not perched on the second-to-top rung of an extension ladder.

"It's still a little crooked."

A few feet away, atop another ladder, Gracie's assistant Jillian blew out an impatient breath. The metal frame underneath her wobbled slightly.

Gracie made an executive decision. "Here is fine. Go ahead and tie it off, Jillian."

Her co-worker looped the gold fabric edging around the corner of a nail and secured a double knot with a flourish. Gracie did the same to her side then climbed shakily to the ground. She glanced up at the front of the aquarium and winced. It *was* a tad crooked, but who really cared? The point was, the public now knew about the special showing of the penguin movie and the discount available. The board of directors had even gone a step further than Gracie had hoped and arranged for all the funds of that particular afternoon viewing to go directly to the gala budget.

They just might just pull this off, food poisoning and all.

Gracie turned to her assistant. "Thanks for all your help, Jillian."

"No problem." Her co-worker smiled at Gracie, sent a withering glance at Lori and then disappeared inside the lobby doors.

"What?" Lori blinked innocently.

"I think you like causing trouble." Gracie moved toward the ladder to fold it back into place.

"Hey, you said to let you know when it was straight." She tilted her head and peered up at the banner. "And for the record, I never did say when."

"I'd rather it be slightly off center than risk losing an arm—or my assistant." The metal screeched as Gracie fought the safety lock. She winced.

"Give me that." Lori helped her with the ladder and together they carried it back inside the aquarium. "So, where's Music Man when you need him?"

"What do you mean?" Gracie glanced over her shoulder to make sure they weren't about to scratch the wall with their wide load.

Lori tossed her hair out of her eyes. "Backward to your left.

You're almost to the maintenance closet." She cleared her throat. "I meant where are a few muscles when we can use them?"

Probably somewhere with Tawny. Gracie adjusted her grip on the ladder as she moved backward around the hallway corner. "Not my place to keep up."

Lori stopped walking. "Are you still mad about what Carter said?"

Gracie tugged at her end. "Keep moving. This isn't exactly light." She glared at Lori's quirked eyebrow and cocked hip. "No, I'm not mad. It's no big deal."

"No big deal, except, you're still mad."

Gracie sighed. "The truth came out, that's all. He has feelings for Tawny." Jealousy flickered in her stomach and she tugged on the metal a second time. "Come on, we're almost there."

"He said that?" Lori took a small step forward then stopped again.

"Not in so many words."

"How many words then?"

Gracie dropped her end of the ladder on the ground and planted her hands on her hips. "He defended her. What else am I supposed to think? Besides, he lied about his dad, why not lie about Tawny?"

Lori's face remained impassive. "Huh. Okay, let's go."

"What? All that and *now* you want to keep moving?"

Lori set her end on the ground with a bang. "Girl, you don't know how good you have it. My ex-fiancé cheated on me, bragged about it and didn't give one crawfish tail if I forgave him or not. Carter is a good guy and he's going to come around, mark my words. He'll show up and apologize for the fight, and you'll forgive him and move right along, Tawny-free. Now, let's get this ladder moved before I break another nail."

"I don't think it's going to be that easy." Gracie reluctantly picked up the heavy extension ladder again and moved a few more steps backward. The closet was just behind her to the right. She side-stepped to allow room for Lori to swing around the hall corner. "Not after what we both said."

"I'm sure you've each heard worse. You're friends—friends are supposed to fight sometimes." Lori helped Gracie walk the ladder into the closet.

"Right. Friends." Gracie shut the maintenance door and leaned against it.

"Tawny is not a threat. Trust me."

"How can you be sure?"

Lori smiled and pointed to the end of the long hallway. "Because look who's coming to apologize?"

Carter fought the urge to run the other direction at Gracie's blank expression as she saw him walking down the hall. Man, he'd give anything to be able to read her movements like he used to. Then the blank canvas switched to dark as her eyes narrowed. He swallowed. Then again, maybe not.

He nudged Andy. "Are you sure this couldn't wait?"

"Gracie needed me to pick up the reimbursement check from the cookout disaster. Do *you* want to tell the church treasurer to wait?" Andy waved at the girls, who lingered at the end of the hallway.

Carter winced as Gracie whispered something to Lori before crossing her arms over her chest. Probably best not to know what was just said. "You could have told me you were stopping here first before you dragged me with you. What happened to getting gumbo?"

"It's next, I promise. I know you guys had a fight but, dude, just give me a second." Andy blew out his breath as they neared Lori and Gracie, still waiting for them by the maintenance closet. "Its awkward enough taking money from Gracie—don't make this worse."

Worse. Right. Andy wasn't the one who had to look Gracie in the eye after having absorbed her verbal assault Sunday night. Though he supposed in hindsight, he hadn't exactly spoken wisely, either.

"Hey, there. Sorry I'm late—had to pick up some baggage." Andy elbowed Carter in the ribs with a grin.

"No problem. The check is in my office. It's right down

here." Without a single glance at Carter, Gracie led Andy down the hall and around the corner.

Carter looked at Lori. She held up her hands in defense. "I don't know a thing."

He waited.

"Okay, I know you guys argued and she's mad and you're annoyed but—"

"Annoyed?" That was putting it mildly, although the hurt kept threatening to submerge the anger. Nothing could drown out the replay of Gracie's words in his head, however. They grew louder with every passing day. *Why can't you just be more like your father?* The irony struck him with a flesh blow and he clenched his fist.

"If not annoyed, then frustrated? Whichever word you prefer, it's ridiculous. You guys have come a long way to fight over something so petty." Lori shrugged. "But, hey, it's your choice. Not mine."

"I'm not so sure any of this is my choice." Carter ran his hand down the length of his face. *Hurry up, Andy.* His stomach growled, and he felt like growling with it. He didn't need advice from Lori right now. She would naturally take Gracie's side, and the last thing he wanted was a game of two against one. He braced himself for a lecture.

"She'll be all right."

Carter's hand dropped from his face. "Huh?" No argument on behalf of her best friend? No biased words of wisdom to help Gracie win?

"You guys will work it out."

"You seem so confident about that." He hooked his fingers in his belt loops and glanced over his shoulder where Gracie had disappeared. "How do you know?"

Lori smiled. "I know Gracie. She won't hold a grudge for long."

Then she must not know about the time Gracie didn't speak to him for three weeks after he convinced her to cover for his skipping P.E. and she ended up with a month of Saturday detentions.

He swallowed the wave of memory. "I know Gracie, too—and I'm not so sure." After all, she'd held this one for seven years.

Gracie handed Andy the church's refund check, fighting the urge to snatch it back from his grip and plead for mercy. "Here you go."

"I really appreciate this, Gracie. If it was my choice, I'd write it off, but…" His words trailed away, and he shrugged. "What can you do?"

"It's not your fault everyone got sick." It wasn't hers, either, but that wasn't the point. She crossed her arms to keep from grabbing at the slip of paper as he folded the money into his shirt pocket.

"Things will work out. You've just got to have faith."

"I do." She tried to smile but the negative balance glaring from the gala's checkbook registry made it feel like more of a grimace.

Andy rested one hip against her desk. "You've still got the fund-raising event this weekend here at the aquarium. That will help get you back on track financially."

"Unless people trip walking in the door and decide to sue."

"Hey, now. You're not usually this negative." Andy leaned down and caught her gaze with his. "What gives?"

Gracie plopped down in her office chair with a sigh. "It's personal."

"I'm a person."

"You're the best friend of the person. That's the problem."

"So my advice is biased? I'm a pastor, Gracie. Give me a few more props than that." Andy tilted his head to one side. "Try me."

Gracie worked her lower lip between her teeth.

"I already know you and Carter had an argument."

Gracie spun a slow half circle in her chair. "He lied to me."

"No, he didn't."

She jerked the chair back around to face him. "What happened to the unbiased part?"

"Carter and I go back to freshman year in college, remember? We had our share of talks. I can promise you his dad was the main reason Carter left Benton." Andy hesitated a beat. "It's all true."

Gracie's feet slammed on the floor, abruptly stopping her chair's motion. The office seemed to tilt beneath her shoes and she drew a ragged breath. Reverend Alexander? The concept seemed too foreign to grasp.

"The gambling, the lies, the cover-ups, the guilt-driven contributions…" Andy lifted one shoulder in a helpless shrug. "The abuse."

"No." The word hissed through her lips but she couldn't deny it any longer. "I can't believe it. Reverend Alexander was like a surrogate dad to me. His sermons were so inspiring, so moving—"

"He was a good performer, Gracie. I'm sure there's probably more that Carter never told me—but I can assure you he wasn't lying the other night."

Why can't you be more like your father? Her own words rang in her mind and she winced at the brutal blows Carter must have felt. Guilt beat a steady rhythm against her heart, and she felt like sinking into the deepest tank in the aquarium. "Why didn't he tell me sooner?"

Andy raised one eyebrow. "Would you have believed him?"

Chapter Twenty-Two

Gracie needed courage—and more butter. She tapped her popcorn bag on her leg, hoping to mix the greasy pieces with the dry. Carter sat two seats to her right in the darkened movie theater, and now, she had no idea where the story line in the movie was going.

Andy and Lori had separated her and Carter's chairs as if they were all still in high school and afraid a fight might break out. Members of the youth group filled the rest of their row and the seats in front of them. Several of the teens had complained Wednesday night at the youth service about watching a documentary, but most of them showed up anyway after Andy announced popcorn was on him. Thankfully, Tawny had stayed home from this fund-raiser, claiming she had to work and would see them all at the gala—she'd be one less thing to distract Gracie from the movie.

A waddling baby penguin filled the wide screen, and several of the children in the audience laughed. Gracie stole a glance sideways. Would Carter even be willing to listen to an apology, should she muster up the courage to offer one? She probably owed him that much—but Andy's confirmation of the truth about Carter's dad still rang unbelievable to her shocked heart. It was hard to grasp a completely new image of the one man in her life who'd always been there for her.

Reverend Alexander had been the only father Gracie knew—and bailed her mother out on more than one occasion financially. Was all his extra money from gambling? The utility bills he often paid for Gracie's mom, the envelopes full of cash he left in their mailbox, the large contributions to the aquarium. If he'd lived such a successful double life, what else had he kept hidden from his congregation? But what kind of man gave to charity at the emotional sacrifice of his own family?

The penguins shuffling on the screen brought a smile to Gracie's face despite her reservations. Even if the Reverend's motivations were wrong, God had a purpose in her being here. It was evident in the joy on the faces around the theater, and hopefully would prove more so when the penguins from upstate were happily settled in their new home at the aquarium. She just might have to rethink the name of the new wing.

Assuming the gala was even somewhat successful.

"Are you going to share that popcorn or what?" Lori's offended whisper pierced Gracie's thoughts.

She automatically held the bag toward her friend. "Don't take all the buttered pieces."

"I wouldn't dream of it." Lori shoved a handful of fluffy kernels into her mouth. "Hey, guys, want some?" She lowered her voice as she passed the bag to Andy and Carter.

"No thanks." Carter's husky whisper tore at Gracie's stomach, and she folded her arms across her middle to stop the quivering. Would he ever cease to affect her like that? *Take a hint, Gracie, it's not meant to be.* But the memory of his kiss stuck in her brain like bread pudding to her ribs, demanding a single thought—what if? What if Tawny was only a threat to the world of interior designing, and not to Gracie's friendship with Carter? What if she'd blown everything out of proportion, *à la* her high school days, and misunderstood Carter's loyalty?

Gracie swallowed hard as she stared at the movie and tried to focus on the male and female penguins braying their intentions to each other.

What if she never got the nerve to find out?

* * *

Carter shifted in the dark theater, wishing he were sitting beside Gracie instead of Andy, who smacked popcorn like a six-year-old. He leaned forward, pretending to adjust the leg of his jeans over his boot, and used the opportunity to sneak a glance at Gracie. Her eyes were focused on the screen, the changing light flickering shadows across her face. More than likely, she hadn't thought twice about him today, other than earlier when he accidentally stepped on the back of her shoe walking up the stairs to their seats.

When was the last time they'd seen a movie together in a theater? Probably a few weeks before his disastrous senior party, where the drama they created on the pier outside his parent's house more than outweighed the conflict in the film. Even then she'd affected him—her teasing smile as she tossed popcorn during the previews, her fake pout when he stole one of her gummy bears. He'd been too dumb to see it.

And just when Carter thought things were finally starting to be made right between them—almost a decade later than they should have—he'd ruined it. Again. Why hadn't he just kept his mouth shut about Tawny? He had no reason to defend her, other than Gracie's suspicions seemed way out of character. If he hadn't been sick and running on almost zero sleep, he'd probably have handled the situation better. Whether Gracie's suspicions were shaded by jealousy or fact, he should have just nodded and found a way to make her smile.

It used to be so easy.

He waved off the bag of popcorn Andy held out to him, too distracted to eat. If Carter hadn't started the argument about Tawny, the truth about his father wouldn't have slipped out. In a way, it was freeing to finally be relieved of the secret. But knocking a dead man off a pedestal was hard to do, deserved or not. Of course, it didn't make much difference since Gracie refused to believe him. Carter shook his head. It was almost as if his dad was getting the last word, even now. He hated how Gracie was working so hard to honor a memory that was a farce.

On the screen, a baby penguin slipped on an icy patch and rolled a few feet in the snow before squawking a protest at its mother. Gracie's laugh mingled with the others around him and tugged at Carter's heart. In that moment, he knew he wanted to hear that laugh every day for the rest of his life. He had to find a way to make up for their fight, a way to show Gracie how he felt about her—insecurities, paranoia, jealousy and all. Maybe a surprise at the gala?

He leaned back in his seat, trying to ignore Andy's loud munching beside him, and narrowed his eyes at the screen. A dozen ideas raced through his mind until one settled and stuck. Carter smiled. It just might work.

Gracie crumpled her empty popcorn bag and tossed it into the overflowing trash bin on her way out of the theater. Ahead of her, Carter, Andy and several of the youth-group members walked, talking and gesturing together. Andy seemed to be imitating one the penguins from the movie, waddling along until Lori laughingly shoved him into the wall.

Haley fell into step beside Gracie. "Men are so weird." She motioned to Carter, who was now doing the penguin walk with Andy.

Gracie laughed. "Just wait."

"It gets better?" Haley raised hopeful eyes to meet hers.

"I didn't say that." Gracie nudged her with her hip.

"I guess they're worth it. Sometimes Jeremy does the stupidest things, then he'll do something really sweet like bring me a latte before school, so I have to forgive him." Haley tucked a stray hair from her ponytail behind her ear and shrugged. "I guess that's how it is with Carter, huh?"

Gracie stopped walking. "What do you mean?"

Haley turned to face her, stepping out of the flow of people exiting the theater. "I can tell you and Carter are totally into each other. It's so obvious." She wrinkled her nose. "I just don't understand why you try to keep it a secret."

"There's no secret. We're not dating." Gracie's heart thumped loudly in her chest. "We're just friends, we go back a long way."

"Right." Haley rolled her eyes. "And me and Jeremy are just friends, too."

Gracie pressed against the wall to make room for a woman pushing a stroller. "It gets complicated when you're older."

"Nothing is more complicated than being a teenager. Trust me." Haley blew at her bangs. "Don't you remember?"

Gracie remembered, all right. The torrent of emotions, the insecurity, the wondering about statuses of friendships versus relationships—come to think of it, not much had changed at all.

"You're a smart girl." Gracie looped her arm around Haley's shoulder and walked her toward the rest of the group waiting by the aquarium front doors. "Jeremy's fortunate to have you."

"Of course he is." Haley stuck her nose in the air, then grinned. "And Carter is fortunate to have you."

Gracie opened her mouth to argue, then shut it slowly. It was pointless to explain. In Haley's mind, Gracie and Carter were already halfway down the aisle at the church—a concept that grew on Gracie more and more with every step she took toward him.

They joined the rest of the youth group and stepped outside into the crisp Saturday air. Lori immediately joined Gracie's side, jabbering about how full the theater was and how they should bring in a great profit, but all Gracie could do was watch the way the December afternoon sun lit Carter's face and lightened his hair.

He shoved his long sleeves halfway up his arms before pausing to play an air guitar with a few of the boys. In the weeks they'd worked together, he'd become a natural with the youth. They looked up to him, and not just because of his former fame—because he understood them. Sometime over the last few weeks, he'd become a part of them—and he was making a difference. What a change from the man Gracie knew in Benton.

Her stomach twisted and she fiddled with the strap of her purse. She had to find a way to tell Carter she was sorry for their fight, and tell him the truth that was becoming more and more evident in her heart. She was ready to consider renewing their friendship—and more. Maybe she could tell him the good news at the gala. She'd be swamped the next week with last-minute preparations and setting up, so she'd use that time to pray about her decision and make sure she was doing the right thing.

Yes, the gala would be great timing. She had a new dress, and the entire evening would serve as the perfect backdrop for the revelation of her heart.

Gracie pressed her fingers against her lips, remembering their kiss from just days ago. Perfect timing or not, would he forgive her for her harsh comments? She still flushed every time she thought about the way she'd spouted off without having all the facts. But how could she have all the facts if he'd kept them from her all these years?

It was getting hard to know who to trust. If the reverend had lived a successful double life, then who was to say Carter wouldn't do the same?

Gracie tried to focus on a teen girl who suddenly clamored for her attention, but her mind kept drifting. Potential rejection or not, trust issues or not, she had to try. All her life she'd felt like she owed others. This time, she owed it to herself.

Chapter Twenty-Three

Gracie surveyed the ballroom at the *Château de Sommeil* with a critical eye, her ever-present clipboard clutched in her arms. Was she forgetting something? The caterer had been paid. They'd raised just enough money from the movie fundraiser to pay for the remaining decorations. Part of Carter's check would have to come from her own personal savings account, but it'd be worth it. They were too close to their goal to admit failure now.

Besides, it was too late. In about seven hours, the banquet room would be filled with the city's elite, dressed in their finest attire and sipping sparkling drinks and hopefully enjoying Carter's performance enough to donate over and above the cost of their tickets.

Gracie made a check mark on her list with her favorite purple pen. It was all finally coming together, but she couldn't shake the sense of foreboding hovering over her head like a looming storm cloud.

"Gracie, go home and relax while I finish this up." Lori, up to her elbows in white linen, draped one of the cloths over a round table and gestured with her head toward the back of the room. "Some of the girls from the youth group have promised to decorate the tree, and my stepmom will be here any minute with the poinsettias. She'll help me with the centerpieces."

"I don't know." Gracie pulled in her lower lip and cast a quick glance around. Circular tables and chairs filled the bulk of the room, except for an empty space near the back where the hotel staff assured her the buffet would be set up well before the start of the party. Surely there was something she needed to do…

"Gracie, go." Lori grabbed another tablecloth, fanning the white material out with a flourish until it settled with a gentle whoosh around the next table. "You've been here all day. Take a bubble bath and a nap, then put on that amazing dress you bought and get back here no sooner than forty-five minutes early."

Her eyes widened. "Forty-five minutes? But what if—"

Lori dropped the next tablecloth and moved to Gracie's side. "It'll all work out." She draped an arm over Gracie's shoulders and began to usher her toward the exit. "Carter will be here in a few hours to warm up. The decorations are handled. The food is prepared. Everything is fine."

"I'm just so afraid something will go wrong. These guests are paying good money to buy a ticket to attend—what if they all want refunds afterward? What if the penguins don't get their funding and this was all for nothing?" A lone tear slipped down Gracie's cheek. She was completely overreacting, but her nerves were shot. Not only that, but what if Carter rejected the speech she'd written that shared her feelings? What if—

"None of those things will happen." Lori squeezed Gracie's hand with both of hers. "Now, go home and take a nap, before my stepmother arrives and starts bossing both of us around."

"A bubble bath does sound good." Gracie picked up her purse from the chair by the door. "Okay, but I'm coming back at least an hour early."

"Fine. But you have to give me your clipboard." Lori held out her hand.

"What?" Gracie's fingers tightened around it. "I've had this with me nonstop for the last week."

"Exactly." Lori pried the board from her fingers. "It'll be right here waiting for you when you get back."

"You're brutal." Gracie wiped away the traces of tears from her face and managed a smile. "But thanks for helping me."

"No problem. You can even use my vanilla bath bubbles, under the bathroom sink."

"I knew I was your best friend for a reason."

Carter eased the razor over the edge of his chin, then tapped the excess white foam into the sink. His hand shook, and he gripped the razor tighter. *Get it together, man.* He couldn't impress Gracie tonight with bits of tissue stuck to his face. He had stage fright, but not the kind he was used to. No, tonight would be different. Tonight, hearts would be on the line—including his.

He ran the blade down his cheek in smooth, even strokes, eyes focused on his reflection in the mirror. His mind, however, already had him standing on stage, singing Gracie the song he'd written for her so many years ago, back when he first started to regret having put out the light in those blue eyes of hers. Tonight, after she heard his performance, she'd meet him at the side of the stage, face glowing, arms open and—

The blade nicked his cheek. Carter winced. A stream of blood trickled over his damp skin, and he pressed a wet cloth to the wound. So much for avoiding the shred of tissue. But the slight burn was nothing compared to the anticipation of seeing Gracie, of convincing her that they could make their relationship work if they just communicated a little better and let go of the past.

A few more of those kisses probably wouldn't hurt, either.

He dropped the rag in the sink and resumed shaving. It still bothered him that Gracie thought he would lie to her face about his dad, but given the circumstances, he realized he couldn't hold a grudge. He'd blasted the information at her in the middle of an argument—not exactly the best time to reveal life-altering details of the past. He was determined to put their misunderstanding behind him, starting tonight. This evening would go perfectly for her. It had to, it was his last chance to impress her. If he didn't succeed this time, Gracie wouldn't give him another opportunity—he knew that as surely as he knew the chords to "Sweet Home Alabama."

Carter wiped all traces of lather from his face and dabbed on a bit of aftershave. *All right, Lord, tonight is up to You. I'm just going to be honest, but I can't make Gracie trust me. Help me remember the music I'm playing, help me remember the words I want to speak to her—and, oh, yeah, help me remember to breathe.*

He moved to the closet door for his tuxedo, still hanging in the plastic bag. Only for Gracie would he wear such a getup. He was going to look like one of her penguins. With a sigh, he looped the black tie around his neck and peered into the mirror, holding each end of the silky material and wishing he could he remember which way the bunny went. A quick glance at his watch set off the conga line of nerves in his stomach. Two hours before the start of the gala, one hour before he needed to run a sound check.

Three hours until he'd know whether or not his future would include his best friend.

Gracie nodded her thanks as a hotel staff member of the *Château de Sommeil* pulled open the double doors to the ballroom. She stepped inside and gasped, the small black purse in her hand falling to her side. To think she had been worried…

Lori had somehow managed to transform the simple, empty space into an elegant Christmas wonderland. Each table centerpiece held a small hurricane lamp, the light within sending flickering shadows across the pristine tablecloths and illuminating clusters of holly and red berries. Black-and-white place settings completed the formal look, along with a red bow tied behind each chair. The stage at the front of the room was trimmed with fluffy piles of glittery cotton to resemble snow, which also helped hide the mass of wires connecting the sound equipment to the speakers.

Gracie's gaze swept to the ceiling. Sparkling silver snowflakes dangled from clear wires, except in the back corner of the ballroom, where a Christmas tree at least ten feet tall commanded attention. Red-and-black ornaments graced the thick branches, and piles of elegantly wrapped gifts filled the space underneath.

But the best part by far were the giant black-and-white printed photographs of Huey, Gumbo, Ernie and the rest of the entire gang, blown up to portrait size and propped on easels placed strategically around the room.

"Gracie! You're back, and only forty-five minutes early after all." Lori joined Gracie's side, the hem of her sparkly red dress swishing around her knees. "What do you think of my work?"

"It's amazing." Gracie couldn't stop staring. "I'm in awe— and the penguin pictures!" Tears formed and she blinked rapidly in an effort to save her makeup. "Perfect touch."

"I thought so." Lori crossed her arms over her chest, sending a satisfied look around the ballroom. "I wanted to surprise you."

"How'd you do all this in one afternoon?"

"I told you, I had a lot of help." Lori ticked off the names on her fingers. "Andy, Haley, Jeremy, the twins, my stepmom…"

"I can tell." Gracie hugged her friend. "I appreciate it more than you know."

"I hope you can relax now. Though it might be hard." Lori pulled away and pointed toward the stage with a grin. "Carter is over there, setting up."

Gracie followed her friend's gesture to Carter, adjusting the microphone stand beside the piano. Her breath caught in her throat—he was wearing a tuxedo. The dark curls of his hair flipped slightly over the sides of a white collar, and the top of his black leather shoes glared under the stage lights.

"I know, right?" Lori shook her head. "Shouldn't be legal to look that good."

Good didn't even come close. Gracie realized her mouth gaped and she shut it with a snap, trying to ignore the nervous twinge in her stomach. She could do this. She just had to remember the speech she'd practiced over and over again in the bubble bath. It was just Carter, after all. She'd never had trouble telling him how she felt before.

She just wouldn't think about the last time she tried to offer him her heart.

Lori squeezed Gracie's hand. "Why don't you grab something to eat before the guests arrive? It'll be hectic for you after that. They just set up the buffet and the spinach dip smells delicious."

"Maybe just a bite. Want to join me?"

"Later. I need to check on a few things first."

"Isn't that my line?" Gracie allowed Lori to turn her toward the food.

"Maybe, but I still have your clipboard." Lori laughed and gave her a gentle shove. "Go eat. I'll find you in a few."

Gracie headed toward the buffet and filled a plate with a few appetizers; careful not to choose anything that would become stuck in her teeth. She would hate to greet guests and thank them for coming with a wad of spinach or a strawberry seed in full view. She reached for a cheese stick lying in the metal warmer and drew back when a hand appeared in her line of vision.

"Let me." Carter reached for her plate and held out a cheese stick clasped in tongs. "You look beautiful." He handed back the dish, his eyes darting down the length of her dress and back to meet her eyes. "Green was always your best color."

"Thanks." She licked her dry lips and looked down at the food in front of her, which was suddenly a blur of colors and textures. *Breathe, just breathe.* She opened her mouth to speak but her intentions stuck in her throat. She couldn't remember the first word of her speech, couldn't even remember her own name. She cleared her throat and tried again. "Carter, I—"

"Gracie, there you are!" Jillian rushed to Gracie's side, her eyes panicky under layers of smoky eye shadow. "We have a problem. You have to come with me, *now.*"

Gracie handed Carter her plate. He took it with an understanding smile. "We'll talk later."

She managed a disappointed nod before allowing Jillian to pull her away. Probably best not to confess her heart's inner desires over a plate of cheese sticks, anyway.

Chapter Twenty-Four

Carter played a dramatic arpeggio down the length of the piano keys as a flourish to "O Holy Night." The crowd of men and women, dressed in their holiday finest, applauded from their seats at the decorated tables. Tawny sat closest to the stage, her leopard-print dress a startling contrast to the subtle attire around her. Gracie had gotten discount tickets for several members of the church, including Tawny and Andy. She said it was the least she could do after all their help in giving the gala a fair chance—a fact that made Carter proud of Gracie, since she still seemed convinced Tawny was somewhat responsible for the cookout disaster.

Tawny beamed at Carter from her table, crossing her legs and winking at him. He nodded slightly in acknowledgment of her, then averted his eyes to his watch. He'd been playing an hour—time for his first break of the evening. He'd grab a glass of punch and then prepare for Gracie's surprise.

He stood from the piano bench, glad to see Tawny caught in conversation with an elderly gentleman. Maybe he could escape to the buffet before she claimed his attention. He quickly turned on the prepared music of instrumental Christmas carols and made his way off the stage. After he'd helped Gracie with her plate earlier in the evening, he'd only seen her again from a distance. She hurried from one end of the banquet room to the other, flanked by her assistant who wore a constantly stressed expression. Gracie, however, always managed to look calm and elegant in that green dress of hers. He wished he'd been able to admire her longer before her co-worker had whisked her away.

Carter poured frothy punch into a cup and took a sip, surveying the room over the rim of the glass. Gracie must have been called away on another emergency—he'd kept an eye out for that flash of sparkling jade, and it was nowhere to be seen. She better get back quick, or he'd have to postpone his surprise.

Nerves mingled in his stomach along with the punch and he set his half-empty glass on a passing attendant's tray. He should have rehearsed more—but no amount of practice could guarantee the response he needed from Gracie. Would she remember the song's meaning and be touched? Or would it just serve as a reminder of all the things that had gone wrong between them?

He should have thought this through better.

Lori approached the buffet table, all smiles. "Hey, Music Man. You're doing a great job up here." She offered a high five.

"Thanks." Carter fought the urge to brush his palms down the legs of his tux before slapping her hand with his. Those stage lights were hot—and thoughts of his upcoming special performance had him soaking wet under his shirt collar.

"This is a great turnout. I think we're really going to pull it off." Lori glanced around the room. "Where's Andy?"

Carter shrugged. "I saw him a little while ago from the stage, standing over here finishing off the last of the Natchitoches meat pies."

"Figures." Lori rolled her eyes with a grin. "Did he have a hollow leg in college, too?"

"He *was* hollow in college. I had to hide my Twinkies."

"I'll remember that next time I bring desserts for the youth." Lori laughed. "What about Gracie? Have you seen her lately?"

Carter shook his head. "I was actually just looking for her."

"Oh, really?" Lori's head cocked to one side, and a knowing smile lit her eyes.

Carter swallowed hard. "Break's over. I better get back up there." He couldn't stand here any longer and keep his mouth shut. He felt an urgency to tell someone of his plan, to get assurance he was doing the right thing in singing Gracie that song—but he had to risk it on his own. He had to go all or nothing, as Gracie had done for him seven years ago.

After a quick goodbye to Lori, Carter made his way back toward the stage, heart hammering a shaky rhythm in his throat. He just hoped Gracie chose the all over the nothing.

Gracie wanted to pull her hair out, but bald hardly went with her dress. Instead, she closed her eyes and drew a deep breath, counting to ten. *I will not fall apart, I will not fall apart.* She opened her eyes. Jillian stood in front of her waiting for an answer, one Gracie still didn't have.

"What should we do?" Jillian asked again, wringing her hands.

Other than run headlong into a wall? Gracie thought fast. "Alert maintenance to the mess in the bathroom and make sure they put the out-of-order sign on the door." And hope no one else needed to use the restroom tonight. The sinks were stopped up—and overflowing—in the ladies' room, and apparently had been for quite some time as there was inches of water on the tile floor. She had a wet black pump as proof of that.

"Right away." Jillian rushed to accomplish her task, the only highlight thus far of Gracie's evening. At least someone was on the ball—but if one more thing went wrong… Gracie had already cleaned up multiple broken ornaments from under the giant Christmas tree in the banquet room, stopped a near fistfight between two waiters who each swore they had been given opposite assignments regarding refreshment refills, and broken two freshly manicured nails. Not only that, but, Huey, who had been backstage in a special cage waiting for his debut moment of being paraded for the thank-you presentation, had disappeared. The cage sat empty, and a hysterical Jillian didn't know where else to look. They'd finally found him in the men's room, and all Gracie could gather was that someone had played a very unfunny prank.

At this point, she more than doubted her decision to share her feelings with Carter. Nothing was going right this evening—why risk further failure?

Gracie fanned at her flushed cheeks and drew another deep breath. She needed to go back inside the banquet room, keep up appearances, but she was half-afraid to open the door for fear of what else might break or explode. She peered inside the glass window of the double doors just as the pre-recorded music snapped off and Carter's voice filled the room via microphone.

"Thank you for your attention this evening." He cleared his throat. "This song is a little different from what I've been playing, so I hope you'll forgive me."

Gracie's mouth dried. What was he up to? He was varying from the song list. *Please, God, no more disasters or bad decisions.* She stepped just inside the doorway of the banquet hall to listen.

Carter stared down at his guitar and began to strum, producing a soft, heartrending vibrato. Then he faced forward with closed eyes and began to sing.

Hey, blue eyes, where have you been?
I've been waiting for you since God knows when.
Hey, blue eyes, where you headed to?
I'd like to tag along if it's all right with you.

Gracie pressed one hand against her stomach, nerves fluttering in time to the music pulsing through the speakers. She hadn't heard this song in years—not after the first time it played on the radio and she nearly drove into a ditch when she realized the title was after Carter's childhood nickname for her. How dare he capitalize on something so personal between them? She'd refused to buy the CD, knowing the song would only serve as constant, bitter reminders of her regrets. But now…now it felt different.

The melody continued, Carter's husky voice growing stronger with each lyric, every word bringing an onslaught on memories that made it difficult to breathe. Carter's grin in the cab of his truck, the dimple that surfaced when he knew he was in trouble, the way the moon on the pier had outlined his silhouette the night her world fell apart. Tears slipped without warning from the corners of Gracie's eyes.

I'll be your knight in shining armor.
I'll be fighting my way to unlock that tower
Where your lonely heart has kept you too many years.

He closed his eyes and played faster, his upper body moving in time to the rhythm. Gracie wanted to run to him, wanted to run away. Wanted to cry and laugh at the same time. She wiped a mascara trail from her cheek with shaky fingers.

I'll be the man you've needed.
I'll be those dreams you've dreamed.

Carter's eyes opened and his gaze collided with Gracie's across the room as he strummed a final chord.

And I'll be your reality.

The words burned straight into Gracie's heart. The stage lights blurred as her eyes filled again, and she didn't even try to stop the cascade of tears as they poured over her lids and onto her cheeks. She had to tell him how she felt—now.

Seven years deserved a second chance.

Carter secured his guitar in its case and cast an anxious glance around the crowded ballroom. Where had Gracie gone? He'd just seen her, standing by the doors of the banquet hall, eyes riveted on him as he strummed the last chords of the song—her song. Had she taken it well? He'd been too far away to accurately decipher her expression, but he hoped the shiny tracks down her cheeks were tears of happiness, not regret.

He'd find out soon enough—if he could figure out where she went. Maybe her assistant had dragged her away to handle another gala issue. He hurried down the stage steps and around the maze of wires and speakers to the back doors.

The air in the empty hallway felt cool against his clammy skin. He wiped a trickle of sweat from his temple and winced. Not exactly the impression he wanted to give, but there wasn't much he could do about it now. He had to find Gracie, before anything else got in his way.

The doors at the other end of the hall opened with a hollow bang and high heels sounded against the terrazzo floor. Carter smiled and turned with anticipation.

"There you are." Tawny's purr matched the print of her dress as she sidled up to him. "Amazing performance, as always."

Carter's heart dropped in his chest. Tawny—not Gracie. He eased back a step as she came closer. "Thanks. Have you seen Gracie?" No use in letting Tawny wonder about his intentions. His days of being polite—and subconsciously misleading—were over.

A slight frown tilted her arched brows. "Not in an hour or so."

"I need to find her."

"Wait." Tawny's arm linked through his and tugged. "What's the rush?"

"I need to talk to Gracie."

"We need to talk, too." A seductive smile curved the red fullness of her lips. "I haven't stopped thinking about you since you walked into *L'Eglise de Grace*. I think it was destiny." She inched forward another step, eyes wide and seemingly innocent behind an abundance of thick lashes.

"Tawny, I—"

"I know it might seem sudden, but I've felt this way since the moment I first heard you on the radio." She pressed forward against his arm, her face inches from his. The heady, spicy aroma of her perfume teased his senses.

"Tawny—" He swallowed hard.

"Don't say it. I feel it, too." She leaned in and the next thing he knew, her lips were on his, her arms snaking around the waist of his tuxedo coat.

A muffled gasp pierced Carter's muffled thoughts, freeing him into action. He pushed Tawny away, grimacing against the chemical remains of her lipstick, and turned.

Gracie.

No. Carter tried to speak, but the words choked in his throat. He held up one hand, begging her to wait, but she backed away, shaking her head so furiously her hair flipped in her eyes. But not before he saw the warning they held. His heart hammered and he opened his mouth to try again. "Gracie, it's not—"

The fire sprinklers above kicked on. Water sprayed from the ceiling, immediately soaking his suit. Beside him, Tawny shrieked and made a dash for the lobby doors.

Gracie looked up, squinting against the influx of water. Carter stepped toward her, hand outstretched, but the banquet room doors burst open and people filed out, creating a barrier between them. Men and women rushed past, holding their purses and jackets over their heads, yelling and squealing as hotel security tried to direct everyone to the proper exits.

The last thing Carter saw before the crowd carried him away was Gracie standing alone at the end of the hallway, water dripping from her hair and down her face.

Or maybe those were tears.

Chapter Twenty-Five

"I don't believe it." Lori passed another tissue to Gracie. "I'm sure there's an explanation."

"Of course there's an explanation." Gracie sniffed, her nose raw under the fresh tissue. "He hasn't changed a single bit." She threw herself against the couch cushions and crumpled the tissue in her hand. "I'm such an idiot."

"No, you're not."

"Yes, I am." Gracie lifted her gaze, burning from an hour of steady crying, to meet her friend's eyes. "I believed him, Lori. I should have known better." She tossed the used tissue on the coffee table where it landed beside a matching pile—soggy evidence of her heartbreak. She kept alternating between tears of betrayal and tears of relief. She'd left the ballroom to touch up her makeup after Carter's song—and it was a good thing. If she hadn't, she would have never seen the truth.

Fresh anger sprung in her stomach and she tugged the damp hem of her dress farther over her knees. Despite still being wet, neither she nor Lori had changed yet from the gala—at this point, catching a cold would be the perfect culmination to her rapidly deteriorating evening.

"I still think you should give him a chance to explain." Lori crossed her legs, the taffeta under her skirt rustling around her knees.

"What's there to explain?" Bitterness tightened Gracie's throat.

"Appearances aren't always accurate."

"Trust me, there was no mistaking this appearance." Gracie shuddered at the memory. "They were kissing. Not many ways to misinterpret."

Lori frowned. "Are you sure that—"

"Positive."

"But maybe he was—"

"No possible way." Gracie sank farther into the couch, her damp hair pressing against her bare shoulders. She shivered. "The worse part is I was on my way to tell Carter how I felt about him when I saw them together…" Her voice trailed off as new tears claimed her eyes. "I'm so stupid—and to think I had forgiven him for the past."

"Forgiveness is a gift, Gracie." Lori clasped her friend's hands between her own. "You're supposed to offer that gift whether he deserves it or not, whether he's wrong or not."

Gracie yanked her hand free. "Forgive the guy who broke my heart—twice? I don't think so." Jealousy sparked in her stomach and she shifted her gaze to the floor. She knew better—Lori was right. But she couldn't handle the influx of memories. The pain was too raw, too fresh. No matter how sincere their kiss last week had been, it no longer mattered. It had been repeated on another woman.

It was like high school all over again. The crowds, the embarrassment. She'd started the evening both times feeling beautiful and cherished, only to watch Carter fall for someone else. She'd even thought they'd shared a moment from the stage, but she obviously was mistaken. Carter hadn't meant that song for her, he was just singing an old hit—probably trying to win over the crowd.

Too bad it hadn't been enough. She might have been able to forgive him if it had worked. At this point, it'd be almost impossible to get the donations they needed for the exhibit expansion—and all because of a little bad luck.

Gracie twisted her bare toes into the carpet. Maybe it

wasn't luck after all. The bathroom flooding, the broken ornaments, the irate waitstaff, Huey's mysterious disappearance moments before his entrance, the fire-alarm sprinklers…all coincidences? Or was someone trying to sabotage the gala? Maybe her earlier paranoia from the cookout hadn't been paranoia after all. Her eyes narrowed—just one more example of her being right and Carter being wrong. Yet the thought brought little comfort.

The doorbell rang. Lori unfolded herself from the couch. "I'll get it." She stared through the peephole, then pulled away, eyes wide. "It's Carter."

The spark of jealousy flared into an inferno of indignation. "Tell him to forget it." She turned her head away from the door, grateful for the bookcase that would hide her from his view.

"Gracie, I really think you should—"

"Just do it."

Carter might have sung his way back from the past into Gracie's present, but from now on, he would remain history. She pressed her lips together and ignored the painful thumping of her heart, the gentle urging to forgive. She would in due time—when all traces of Carter were, once again, nothing but memories.

Carter figured Gracie would refuse to see him, but he had to try. Lori's cold dismissal proved Gracie had already won one person to her side of the story—his chances of explaining now were probably not favorable.

He turned and edged away from the front door, hands shoved in his wet tuxedo pockets. The porch light even seemed to glare an accusation against his back as he headed slowly down the front walk. His big moment, and he'd ruined it. Why hadn't he seen what Tawny was doing? He should have anticipated her advance, done more to stop it. Of course he hadn't wanted to kiss her, but he wasn't exactly offered much choice—a fact Gracie would never believe.

A breeze tickled under his collar, and he shivered. After the guests had made their abrupt exit and he'd packed up his equipment—which thankfully had escaped ruin from the water by being in its case—he'd found Tawny and begged her to go after Gracie, to explain that it wasn't as Gracie thought. But the hard sheen in Tawny's eyes more than showed what she thought about that idea. If there was any doubt, her pushing past with her chin in the air, mumbling about "rejecting the best thing that'd ever happened to him" about summed it up. How he managed to break two hearts in one night— three, if he counted his own—was still a mystery.

God, this didn't exactly go as planned. Shoulders hunched, Carter glanced both ways before crossing the street in front of the girls' townhouse. The worst part was, he still had no idea how Gracie received his song. What had she been coming to tell him? What would have happened if Tawny hadn't shown up and sunk her claws in before he could escape? He might be sitting with Gracie on her couch right now, drying his hair with a towel, laughing at the bad luck of the evening and whispering plans for their next date. First date, really—one that would never happen now.

He drove back to Andy's apartment. Evening had long since consumed the streets, and the few stars in the dark sky above shone as if they had no idea his night was ruined. He'd lost Gracie—he knew it deep down in the solid part of his soul, the part that knew he should pray but couldn't find the words.

"You all right, man?" Andy met him at the door with a Dr. Pepper and a worried frown.

"Just great." Carter shouldered past him into the living room, loosening his damp tie with one finger. He plopped down on the couch and opened the drink, not even caring if he spilled any on his tux and lost the deposit. Were tuxedos dry clean only? He might have lost the deposit anyway after that random alarm went off and soaked the entire first floor.

Andy slowly shut the front door. "I guess talking to Gracie didn't go very well."

"She won't even let me explain. We're done." He ran his

hand down the length of his face, wincing at the roughness of the stubble on his chin. "I'm done."

"What do you mean?"

"I can't stay here any longer. The gala is over, so my job is over—and I obviously have no reason to stick around for Gracie." Carter took a drag from his can of soda. Just saying her name out loud stung worse than the carbonated fizz sliding down his throat. He drank faster.

"What about the youth at the church? Stay for them." Andy sat down in the recliner. "They still want one more concert out of you, remember?"

Carter shook his head. "They'll forget about it. I didn't do much for them." Coming here had been a mistake. He should have stayed in Benton, maybe hunted around for an intern position at a church. Something, anything other than submitting himself to the heartache—and embarrassing failure—of his time in New Orleans.

"Are you kidding? You did more than you think." Andy leaned forward, the recliner creaking in protest. "Three boys I've been trying to minister to for months said that if someone as cool and as talented as you could give up a famous career for a relationship with God, then they wanted that, too."

Warmth pricked at the icy shell of Carter's attitude. His hands clenched the aluminum can. "They said that?"

"Yep. And now a lot of the kids want to share their own stories after hearing yours. You really got everyone fired up."

"I just sang a few songs, at one concert. How is that possible?"

"You were real with them. You were available, and you didn't push, just showed them who you were. It was enough, man." Andy shrugged. "It doesn't take much with these guys, just someone who's legit."

Carter stared down at his hands. Legit. Honest. Truthful. Ironically, all the things he finally was, but couldn't prove to Gracie. If the guys in the youth group saw those qualities in him, then why couldn't she? Why wouldn't she look past his former mistakes and give him a chance? He thought singing

"Blue Eyes" to her would have revealed his intentions and his heart—but the song must have meant nothing. He must mean nothing.

Carter slowly shook his head at Andy. "I'm sorry, man. I can't stay." He swallowed and looked away. "Not even for the kids."

Gracie tossed under the covers in her bed, unable to get comfortable. Her body was more than tired, but her mind wouldn't stop replaying the disastrous night over and over again. Could anything else have possibly gone wrong?

The fan clicked an annoying rhythm above Gracie's head and she rolled over, pulling the sheet up to her ears. Guilt pressed a heavy burden against her shoulders. Ticket sales of the attendees weren't enough to bring in what the new exhibit cost. Everything depended on the extra donations the guests would have made—and from her last count, they didn't even come close. After all, who wanted to donate to such an unorganized and disastrous event? Probably no one even had time to reach for their checkbooks before the sprinklers went off and cut the evening short. What bad timing for a false alarm.

But maybe it was for the best. She couldn't have faced Carter again in the banquet room, couldn't have listened to his closing song after what she witnessed between him and Tawny. Gracie shuddered and hit her fist into her pillow. Of all the women in the world, why Tawny? Was Carter still that weak toward beautiful women, or was it real attraction and admiration? Gracie wasn't sure which possibility made her stomach churn worse. At least now that the gala was over, he would be leaving and going back to Benton.

Unless he stayed for Tawny.

Reality struck then with startling clarity and Gracie clenched her pillowcase between her fingers. She would never be free of Carter. Whether he stayed in New Orleans or not, his presence left fingerprints on everything she did, on everything she remembered. The man she'd loved in the past had taken over her present, and she was helpless to stop him. He had once again weaseled his way into her life, invading her thoughts, her goals, her hopes for the future.

Tears dripped onto Gracie's pillow and she let them fall, mourning the loss of her dreams and the loss of the only man she'd ever thought she'd give her heart to—the man she'd never be able to trust again with either.

Chapter Twenty-Six

Sunday morning, Carter cornered Tawny as she exited a pew in the back row of the church. "We need to talk."

Tawny's dark, heavily made-up eyes flickered over him and then dismissed him just as casually. "I don't think so. I'm late for a lunch date."

"This is important." Ignoring her protests, Carter took Tawny's arm and steered her to the emptying lobby, near the welcome table. A potted fern partially hid them from view of the families leaving the church, but he picked up a bulletin as a prop in case anyone was paying attention. "You have to talk to Gracie."

Tawny struggled in the grip he had on her elbow, and he reluctantly let go. No use causing a scene in the foyer. "Why in the world would I do that?"

"Because it's the right thing to do. Because you know how upset she is. Because it's not fair to me or to her to let her think what she's thinking." Carter ran a hand over his hair, forgetting it had been gelled for church, and winced at the rough tips. "Please, Tawny?" Gracie had to know the truth before he left. It might not change anything between them, but he couldn't stand the thought of going back to Benton with Gracie believing him capable of hurting her—again.

Tawny flipped her hair over her shoulder. "You really love her, don't you?"

Carter hesitated. He hadn't even been able to tell Gracie his true feelings yet—how could he tell them to someone else first?

"Never mind. It's written all over you." Tawny's voice dripped with disgust. "Sorry to stand in the way of true love and all, but you'll have to figure this one out on your own. It's not my problem."

"Not your—" He drew a deep breath. An elderly man in a gray suit shot them a curious glance as he passed by. Carter lowered his voice. "It is your problem, Tawny. You started the whole thing."

A red tinge crept up Tawny's cheeks. "It was a... misunderstanding."

Clarity dawned, along with a sick feeling in his stomach. All those times he'd been nice to Tawny, trying to reach out as a fellow church member, be a friend when others snubbed her... He swallowed. "You thought I wanted you to kiss me, didn't you?"

Tawny shrugged and fiddled with her leather purse strap.

Carter stepped away, dropping the forgotten bulletin on the table. After all his attempts not to lead Tawny on, somehow he still managed to do just that. Or was the woman just so unaccustomed to hearing "no" that she'd blazed ahead anyway?

He risked a glance at Tawny's ducked head, her hair falling over her face in loose waves, and sighed. Regardless of whose fault it was, Tawny was embarrassed now—which didn't bode well for getting her to do what he needed. What was that phrase about a woman scorned? And now he had two on his hands. *God, a little wisdom at the moment would be great.*

He spoke slowly, to avoid any further confusion. "I'm sorry if I ever gave you the wrong impression about us. That wasn't my—"

"Carter!" Haley and the twins, Lydia and Lana, suddenly approached his side, Bibles clasped against their chests. Jeremy towered right behind them, and he reached over Haley's head to slap Carter a high five. Man, he was going to miss those kids.

"How was the fund-raiser?"

"We want to hear all about it. Did our signs work?"

"Did lots of people show up?"

"Yeah, did the penguins get their money?"

Carter held up his hands against the barrage of questions. "Whoa, hold on a minute. I'm not sure of the final numbers but—"

"Where's Gracie?" Haley interrupted, looking around the nearly empty foyer. Her eyes narrowed.

Carter shot Tawny a pointed look. "She's not here. She must not be feeling well."

Tawny averted her eyes, turning toward the bulletin board that hung above the welcome table.

"Pastor Andy told us this morning there were several problems at the gala, and for us not to get too excited about the end results until they knew for sure." Haley frowned. "What happened?"

Tawny coughed, hard.

"Just a few minor incidents." Carter shrugged. That wasn't exactly true, but he didn't want to upset the youth over potentially nothing. Andy had shared the same concerns about the gala's profits last night. "Nothing ever goes perfectly."

"I heard there was a fire." Jeremy crossed his arms over his chest. "Doesn't sound too minor to me."

"No fire, just a false alarm. The sprinkler system came on, so the night's agenda sort of fell short."

"How short?" One of the twins raised their eyebrows.

The other twin's eyes widened in panic. "Yeah, was all our hard work for nothing?"

"No way!" Haley protested. She began to bounce on the balls of her feet. "I gave up several Saturdays for this gala. Those penguins better get what they need!"

Tawny edged away from the group. "I'm late for a meeting. I'll, um, I'll see you guys later."

"Tawny, wait." Carter took a step toward her as she turned to leave, but Haley and the twin's pleading glances held him back. He shouted after her as she headed down the hall toward the exit. "Will you at least consider what I asked?"

Tawny hesitated at the double doors, her back stiff. Carter held his breath. Was she finally coming around? *Please, Tawny, please...*

Without further response or even a glance back, she pushed open the doors and disappeared into the sunlight.

Gracie flipped through the pages of Psalms, eyes blurred from lack of sleep and too much crying. She should have been in church, but she couldn't bear seeing Carter and Tawny together at the service. So she went to her office at the aquarium instead and sat at her desk with a mug of coffee, trying to focus on her scripture reading. But all she could see on the pages were dollar signs—and there weren't enough of them.

God, I'm a total failure. What am I going to do now? Where are those birds going to go? There wasn't another aquarium in the state that could afford such an addition, especially at the last minute. Hurricane Katrina had affected the entire area—no one had that kind of cash lying around.

She ran her thumb down the gold siding of the Bible, the pages bristling under her finger. A passage in Psalm 130 caught her eye, and she drew a tight breath. *If You, O Lord, kept a record of sins, O Lord, who could stand? But with You there is forgiveness; therefore You are feared.*

Forgiveness. Not exactly what she wanted to hear at the moment. Gracie shut the book with a snap. What had the pastor preached on today at *L'Eglise de Grace?* Had the youth group missed her? They were probably asking a dozen questions about the gala's success—questions that poor Andy would have to dodge until they received the final count of donations from the Board. The paperwork should be on her desk Tuesday morning.

If she survived long enough to see it.

A knock sounded on her open office door, and Gracie jumped, her elbow knocking against her mug of coffee. Drops splattered across the desk.

Tawny stood framed in the doorway, her leopard-print purse on one shoulder, her chin in the air. "May I come in?"

"I—I guess." Gracie wiped up the coffee, hoping her shock didn't show on her face. What in the world was Tawny doing at the aquarium? How'd she even get in? The front doors should have been locked.

"I sweet-talked maintenance into letting me come visit you. Told them I was your sister." Seemingly reading Gracie's mind, Tawny settled into the chair across from her desk and crossed her legs.

"Remind me to have maintenance fired." Gracie bit her tongue, but the phrase slipped out anyway.

Tawny's eyes narrowed. "Look, I know we're not exactly best friends, Gracie, but I have something to say—and it's not easy."

"Sorry." Gracie settled back in her chair, folding her arms over her pounding heart. "Go ahead." Was Tawny just going to brag about her and Carter? If so, Gracie might run from the aquarium, screaming—and probably dump the contents of that stupid leopard-print purse over Tawny's head on her way out the door.

"I was just at the church, and the youth group was asking about the gala." Tawny blew a strand of hair out of her eyes with a huff. "I couldn't take it anymore. They were so upset about how things turned out, after all their hard work, I just—" Her voice trailed off and she tugged at a string on her purse.

Gracie frowned. "I don't understand. Why would you feel bad about the gala being a flop?"

Tawny shrugged one shoulder, picking furiously at her purse.

Understanding sank in with sharp claws. Gracie gasped. "It was you, wasn't it? You've been sabotaging all the fundraisers."

"And the gala itself," Tawny admitted.

"The cookout food poisoning? The lost advertising posters? Huey's random bathroom trip? The fire alarm sprinklers going off?"

She chewed on her overly glossed lips. "Yes."

Gracie shoved her chair back, the wheels screeching in protest.

"I came to say I'm sorry!" Tawny's head jerked up. "I got jealous. You knew I liked Carter, but he…well, he picked you over me."

The news brought both relief and confusion coursing through Gracie's veins. If Carter had chosen Gracie over Tawny, then what about their kiss at the banquet? She shook her head quickly. One issue at a time. "So because you were jealous, you decided to get revenge on me by attacking a good cause?"

Tawny squirmed in her chair. "It sounds so much worse when you put it that way."

Gracie briefly closed her eyes.

"I'm sorry! Look, I'll do whatever I can to help." Tawny pulled her checkbook from her purse. "I can write a check toward your bottom line." She frowned at her register. "Well, not a big one."

"It's too late." Gracie shook her head. "Much too late."

"Surely I can do something."

Gracie set her jaw. "You can leave."

"Do you forgive me?" Tawny's voice dropped to a whisper. "I know it was wrong. I'm just not used to being skipped over." She let out a short laugh. "And I would have gotten away with it if I could stand the thought of those kids being so upset."

Gracie's gaze dropped to her Bible, still lying on the desk in front of her, and remembered the words on forgiveness she'd read just moments before Tawny's arrival. She sighed.

"So, do you? Forgive me?"

Gracie fingered the crimson bookmark on the page. "You upset a lot of people, Tawny. Not just the youth. Your actions reach further than you think." All the way to a closing aquarium in north Louisiana. Gracie's stomach rolled. "But yes, I forgive you. It doesn't exactly fix things, but consider yourself forgiven."

Tawny stood with a nod. "Thank you." She moved to the

door, shoulders slightly hunched, then turned, one hand resting against the frame. "And by the way, just so you know—" She looked down, let out a slow breath, then met Gracie's gaze. "I kissed Carter at the gala, not the other way around."

Gracie's heart stopped, then thudded again in double-time.

Tawny shook her head and offered a sad smile. "He's apparently got this thing for blue eyes."

Chapter Twenty-Seven

"What do you mean, he's gone?" Lori's voice echoed off the walls of the gift shop and she paused in her rearranging of the stuffed-animal display.

"Gone. Disappeared. Vanished." Gracie rubbed her temples with both fingers. "However you want to say it, Carter is no longer in New Orleans." She slumped against the wall near the glass doors.

Lori's eyes widened. "Where'd he go?"

"Andy said back home to Benton."

"And you're not going after him?"

Gracie snorted. "Isn't that supposed to be the other way around?"

"This isn't a Disney movie, this is real life. You want to lose Carter?"

Gracie picked up a stuffed walrus from the shelf and fingered its tusks. "I never had him in the first place."

Lori snatched the animal from Gracie's hands and shook it at her. "Don't even start with me on that. I saw that kiss between you two—and now that Tawny has confessed, you know for sure there is nothing going on with them."

"But Carter knew all those things, too." Gracie grabbed the stuffed walrus and tossed it back on the display. "So tell me this—why did he leave?"

Lori's mouth opened, then closed.

"Exactly." Gracie shut her eyes. Her heart had been slowly breaking ever since she saw Tawny with Carter at the gala. Tawny's confession Sunday had served as a bandage to the wound, but Carter's abrupt departure had ripped it off, revealing not only the original crack underneath but also a sting that burned all the way through.

She'd spent Sunday evening flipping through the pages of her Bible, praying she'd approach Carter with the right words. She had so much to apologize for she didn't know where to begin. What if he refused to forgive her? She'd ignored his attempts at reconciliation, and deserved for him to do the same—she just didn't think she could bear it if he did.

But when she finally muscled up the nerve to call Andy's apartment Monday night, she'd learned the truth. Carter had packed his things and left after the morning worship service Sunday.

Without saying goodbye.

"I don't know what to tell you." Lori opened her arms and drew Gracie into a hug. "I'm really sorry."

Gracie clung to her friend's shoulders, throat tight, determined not to cry. Not over Carter, not anymore. She was through.

Gracie left the gift shop after a few minutes of stalling with Lori, and headed slowly to her desk, her emotions numb. Time to focus. She had a lot to do today—the usual list of chores regarding the care of the penguins, plus the post-gala details, including wrap-up phone calls and thank-you notes to write. And, of course, she needed to go over the financial report from the board—assuming the telltale piece of paper hadn't burned a hole through her desk by now. She'd avoided it first thing this morning when starting her shift, deciding it was much too early in the day for bad news.

But there was no use putting off the inevitable any longer. She shut the office door behind her with a soft click. The numbers waited in a blue folder in the center of her desk. She drew a deep breath and settled back in her chair, fingering the edge of the file folder. *God, let us be close. That's all I ask.* Then maybe she could find another way to make the impossible possible—ask for an extension, see if the penguins from upstate could go somewhere else temporarily, or maybe convince the board to take out a short-term loan until she held a few more fund-raisers.

But even as the ideas swam around her mind, she knew it didn't matter. As much as the higher-ups loved the penguins and all the animals in the aquarium, it was still a business—and money had to come first.

She opened the folder with a quick flip of her wrist. *Better to get it over with.* Her eyes skimmed the rows of figures until they settled on the bottom number. Gracie blinked. They'd made it.

"How—what—" Gracie followed the rows of numbers with her finger, shaking her head. It didn't make sense. Someone had to have made a simple mathematical mistake...no, there. Her finger stopped on the second to last figure, and so did her heart.

An anonymous donation, in the exact amount they needed to meet their goal.

The wooden boards creaked beneath Carter's feet. He stood with his back to the wind, staring out over the ripples of water on Black Bayou. The breeze stirred the mossy branches of the cypress trees, and near the shore, a turtle sunbathed on a rock. Everything was peaceful, calm...except his heart.

He shouldn't have come here, not with a dozen memories and even more regrets in his wake, but it was as if his truck had a mind of its own. One minute he was driving toward the post office to mail a bunch of bills, the next he'd turned south and was pulling into his mother's driveway. Thankfully, she wasn't home and he had the pier to himself.

God, did I do the right thing? Carter crouched into a sitting position and dangled his feet over the side of the dock. Right seemed so relative these days. He'd been back from New

Orleans a few weeks now, and not a single word from Gracie. Not that he really blamed her, since he left without saying goodbye. But what could he have said to make everything better? Any explanation, without Tawny backing it up, only sounded like poor excuses. *It's not what you think, it wasn't like that, she means nothing to me*—all read like bad lines from a low-budget movie. If Gracie refused to hear him out, and Tawny refused to tell her side of the story, what hope did he have?

He picked up a rock from the pier and chunked it into the dark water. Carter hoped Andy had delivered his donation check to the aquarium board, and even more importantly, hoped he remembered to keep it anonymous. Hurt as Carter was, he couldn't leave Gracie's gala to failure, not when he had the means to help. He had the money to spare, and while the parting gift did little to erase the bad taste in his mouth, at least it eased a bit of the guilt that burdened his spirit. Of course he hadn't wanted Tawny to kiss him, but she'd admitted she thought he did. He'd unintentionally led her on, and he'd paid for it.

Carter shook his head with a harsh laugh. Years in the music industry offered him more women than he could keep up with, and any interaction in those days certainly hadn't been a misunderstanding. He'd known exactly what he was doing, and never cared who he hurt—even his best friend. Were these the consequences he had to suffer through for his past choices?

Carter leaned back, braced his palms against the sun-warmed boards and narrowed his eyes. Maybe that's how his father felt when he wrote all those checks over the years to the aquarium and other good causes. Did the numbers in his dad's checkbook register eliminate the guilt from living a double life, from keeping secrets and fooling his trusting congregation?

Maybe they were more alike than he thought. Different choices, different sins—same end reaction to the guilt. Except Carter had turned from his past, and moved forward. Had his father made such reconciliation before his death? He'd never know now—and in a way, Carter wasn't sure he wanted to.

Carter stood and dusted his hands on the back pockets of his jeans. The sun shimmered on the water, and a fish splashed amidst the rhinestone sparkles of the wave. One of the last times he'd stood here the moon had teased the tears in Gracie's eyes, making them shine brighter than the stars in the black velvet sky. He remembered every moment of that night, every word spoken—every word he longed to take back. He should have just told Gracie the truth then, told her he was scared but felt the same way she did, told her about his dad and how he couldn't stay, but he'd take her with him if he could. He should have given her something to dash away those tears, instead of offering only his back as he walked away, naive and with too much to prove to all the wrong people.

Carter released a tight breath and reached into his pocket for his keys. No more reminiscing, it'd only make the noose he felt around his neck tighten that much more. He was home now, and had plenty to do other than wish away the future with regrets of the past. He needed to find a job, obtain a fresh start, maybe even date again.

The thought rolled his stomach and he turned abruptly toward his truck. He didn't want anyone else, he wanted Gracie. And not only because her kiss had stirred feelings in him that all the other women in his past combined had never reached—but because she knew him, inside and out, and at one point, had loved him anyway. Unconditional love was something his father had never been able to offer. Carter might not have ever pleased his parents growing up, but once upon a time, he'd pleased his best friend, the woman he took for granted. The woman he knew he needed for the rest of his life.

God, is there any hope for a second chance? Make that a third chance, after the incident with Tawny at the gala. Carter paused on the gravel driveway and closed his eyes, his keys biting into his palm. *Any hope at all?*

The breeze crested then stilled, and even the birds ceased

their chirping from the upper branches of the cypress. The rhythm of the gentle rolling waves behind him lapped an answer from the shore—wait…wait…wait…

Chapter Twenty-Eight

Three Months Later

Gracie surveyed the new penguin exhibit with her hands on her hips. "I can't believe it came together so quickly."

"Hooray for contractors in high places." Lori nudged Gracie's shoulder with her own. "So did you ever find out who that last-minute, anonymous donation was?"

"Probably someone on the board who didn't want to put up with me pouting." Gracie grinned. "I'm not sure who it was, but I definitely am grateful."

After all the months of planning prepping, and praying, the addition was finally complete and the penguins from upstate were already enjoying their new home. Gracie still had trouble believing they had actually pulled it off—though she knew without a doubt they had a little help from above.

Gracie took a step back and admired the newly constructed addition. The entire display had been extended to include another showroom, complete with an even larger water fountain and rock pond. She had fought to give them a water slide, at Lori's suggestion, but the curator of birds said that was taking things a bit far. The aquarium was open this Monday afternoon for a special dedication service, complete with a long red ribbon that stretched across one end of the platform to the other. Gracie would cut it during the ceremony.

"Are you nervous about your thank-you speech?" Lori asked. She giggled as one of the penguins splashed the water behind the glass, inches from her face.

"No. Not yet, anyway." Gracie still didn't enjoy public speaking, but she figured it was the least she could do, given everyone's hard work.

"Give it time." Lori winked. "Are the kids from the church here yet?"

"I'm not sure." It was great of the youth to come out and support the ribbon-cutting ceremony—after all their hard work painting posters and running the various fund-raisers, they deserved to see the fruits of their handiwork. Though it made Carter's absence all the more conspicuous.

Gracie cleared her throat. She'd spent enough time making wishes about Carter. This was a day of celebration, not regrets. "There's a crowd gathered in the lobby. They're keeping everyone in there until two o'clock."

"Cool. So we got a private viewing." Lori tapped the glass with her finger as Gumbo swam by.

"Hey, I practically helped lay down tile. I have the right to be here." Gracie bumped Lori with her hip. "You, however, Ms. Gift Shop…"

"I won't be working that party store for long." Lori bumped her back. "I have dreams, you know." She raised her nose in the air and flipped her long hair over her shoulder.

"Right. How could I forget? Your big dreams of flipping overly processed beef patties." Gracie winked.

"Ha, ha. For your information, I already have—"

"Gracie, are you ready?" Her boss poked his head around the corner of the hallway, interrupting Lori's indignant speech. "They're about to let the crowd in. We need you to move into the exhibit so you can begin your presentation."

Gracie swallowed hard against the sudden burst of nerves that jump-started in her stomach. *God, help me not to make a fool of myself.* She nodded once. "Ready."

* * *

"Are you sure she doesn't know I'm here?" Carter looked over his shoulder, one hand tight against his shirt pocket, hoping to conceal what rode inside. That part no one could know yet—except the youth group who promised to help him pull off the surprise.

Lydia and Lana nodded as one. "You're safe."

Haley reached up and picked a piece of lint off his shoulder. "You'll do great. Don't worry."

"Yeah, man. Just breathe." Jeremy knocked his shoulder into Carter's. "Isn't that an old stage trick or something?" He laughed.

"Something like that." Carter released a tight breath and shook out his arms. "Are you guys ready with the signs?"

The teens held up their cardboard signs, each with an individual letter painted on the front in bold blue strokes.

Carter nodded in approval, then paused. "Wait. Where's the penguin?"

"Huey's in the exhibit, duh." Haley rolled her eyes. "Don't you think Gracie would have noticed him missing?"

Carter shook his head abruptly. Of course she would. "But how—"

"Don't worry, we figured out a plan with Jillian, Gracie's assistant. She's got it all under control." Haley cocked her head to one side. "Are you going to be okay?"

He nodded, but his head felt light. Was he really going to do this? His shirt pocket suddenly felt heavier than the rocks he knew lined the perimeter of the penguin exhibit. *God, please let this work.* He was already risking rejection of his heart—not to mention public humiliation if things didn't go as planned.

Andy pushed through the crowd and joined Carter's side. "You ready for this?" He grinned.

Of course, his friend was excited. He got to stand back and watch. Carter fought the wave of nausea rolling in his stomach. "Hope so." It was too late to change his mind now. Besides, the end result would be worth it—wouldn't it?

"Don't worry about it. You're golden." Andy tilted his head to one side. "Actually, right now you're more like a yellowish green."

Carter opened his mouth to respond, then closed it as a man in a dark suit opened the lobby doors. "Folks, right this way. It's time for the dedication ceremony to begin." He stepped back and the crowd began to file through the doors.

"This is it. Go time." Jeremy clapped him on the back as Andy briefly massaged his shoulders.

Haley straightened the collar of his button-down shirt. "Yeah, go get 'em, Music Man."

The rest of the youth offered words of encouragement as they held their signs behind their backs and filed toward the exhibit. Carter popped his knuckles, exhaled abruptly, and followed them toward what promised to be either certain disaster—or the happiest day of his life.

Gracie smiled and waved discreetly at Andy, Haley and the other members of the *L'Eglise de Grace* youth group from behind the window of the new exhibit. A rush of pride warmed her heart at all they had done to help. Those kids had certainly come a long way from the hardened bunch she met a few years ago when she and Lori first started volunteering. She couldn't wait to give them their promised backstage tour after the dedication. And as a special surprise, she was naming the new wing after the youth group.

She checked the microphone pinned to her shirt, then darted another glance at the gathering crowd—probably a hundred more people than expected. The cake in the lobby wouldn't go far, that was for sure. Teenagers in tank tops, elderly men and women with canes, and middle-aged couples holding tightly to toddlers were stuffed in the hallway, shoulder to shoulder, all smiles as they watched the penguins playing in the water.

Gracie drew a deep breath. *Here we go.* "Hello, and welcome to the Aquarium of the America's new-and-improved penguin exhibit." She went on to explain the circumstances behind the homeless penguins, and how dire the situation had been until the community pitched in and contributed to their new home. The crowd applauded and cheered.

"Are there any questions?" Gracie released her breath, glad the speech part of her program was over. Now she could feed off the crowd and relax while the penguins darted around her feet.

Haley, standing close to the glass with Jeremy, raised her hand. "How can you tell them apart?"

Gracie smiled. "Easy. Spend ten minutes in the exhibit, and you'll see."

The crowd chuckled appreciatively.

"All of the penguins have very distinctive personalities. Some are show-offs, some are shy, some are nice only if they get what they want. Jackson, one of the newbies from north Louisiana, is so eager to please it's almost heartbreaking." Gracie pointed him out from the pack. "It's like he knows he was almost homeless and is eternally grateful." She swiped playfully at the top of Huey's head as he waddled past, beak in the air. "Then, of course, there's Huey here. Can't mistake him with anyone."

She answered a few more questions about the penguin's previous living conditions and how they were adapting to the change, then noticed a hand raised in the back of the crowd, near the wall. The lights from the exhibit silhouetted the person's shape, and she narrowed her eyes, trying to make out distinguishing features. "You there in the back?"

The person stayed in the shadows, but a deep voice carried through the sound system. "I have a question, ma'am."

"Yes?" She tilted her head, still unable to see the man clearly.

He stepped forward, parting the crowd until the aquarium's dim lighting revealed the familiar planes of his face.

Carter.

The lights blurred and shock had Gracie reaching for the window ledge for support. He was here. He came. Her lips parted to speak, but her tongue felt glued to the roof of her mouth. Then she knew—the mysterious donor. All the pieces fell into place, and a gasp froze in her throat. Carter had given that anonymous donation to finish the funding. It was so obvious.

But was it for the penguins and the youth group—or for her?

Words still seemed out of her grasp. Gracie swallowed and tried again, not sure which possibility rattled her the most. "Your, uh—your question?"

Multiple cardboard signs suddenly planted themselves against the glass, a grinning youth group member behind each brightly painted letter.

WILL U MARRY ME?

Gracie's grip tightened on the ledge then slid off, her hand dangling limply at her side. Carter's eyes collided with hers and held, his expression earnest, humble, hopeful. Gracie licked her dry lips, unable to break the gaze that held her fast, unable to breathe, to speak, to move. A million thoughts tumbled through her mind as one tangled knot of emotion—doubt, embarrassment, fear, elation—until a braying from below startled her back into reality.

Huey stood at her feet, wearing a right red collar with a small box tied to the back. Gracie knelt in front of him. "Huey, what are—" Then Jillian edged slowly away from the inside of the exhibit, a big grin lighting her features.

Heat burned Gracie's throat and chest as she slowly untied the string around the black velvet box. Haley's nose pressed against the glass window and she bounced impatiently as Gracie rubbed her fingers over the soft lid. She cracked the edge, then hesitated. If she opened it, this entire dreamlike scenario became real—there would be no going back. Could she reject Carter in front of a group of people?

Could she reject him at all?

The crowd in front of the window had hushed, and the anticipation was thick enough to slice with a chainsaw. Her head felt as if it might burst if she didn't make a decision soon. Logic and emotion warred with each other in an endless battle of possibilities. *We'd kill each other. How can I live without him? He hurt me. He's my best friend.* Then one final thought seemed to piece together the cracks of betrayal still frozen in her heart.

I love him.

Peace rolled over Gracie in gentle waves and she opened the hinged box without further hesitation. A diamond solitaire on a white gold band gleamed a welcome from its black velvet home and she turned eager eyes to the crowd, ready to give Carter her answer.

He was gone.

Her breath tightened and her heart sunk, but then he was there, in the exhibit, kneeling in front her, next to Huey. He took her hand and clutched it against his heart. "Gracie, I know this might seem crazy, but I can't do this anymore. I can't live without my best friend. I need you in my life full-time."

She opened her mouth to give her answer, the answer that bubbled up in her heart in a spring of sudden certainty, but he kept talking.

"I know I've messed up, and I know not everything in my family was as you thought, but I want to make things right with you. With us. You're an integral part of my past and my present—I can't imagine a future without you."

Gracie held up the ring and opened her mouth but again Carter interrupted, his grip on her hand increasing until her fingers tingled. "Will you marry me? Will you be my best friend and my wife and allow me the pleasure of looking into those blue eyes of yours every morning and every night?"

Gracie smiled and slipped the ring on her left finger. "What does this tell you?"

Carter rose slowly to his feet, hope lighting his features and that infamous boyish grin spreading across his face. "Really?"

She looped her arms around his neck, never having felt surer about anything. This was Carter. *Her* Carter—her best friend, her soul mate, her future husband. She knew it as surely as she knew that God was smiling down on them and Lori was making fish faces against the exhibit window behind her back. "Positive."

The crowd outside erupted into applause. Carter leaned down and sealed the commitment with a kiss. Huey squawked at his feet and he pulled away long enough to address the bird. "Huey, man, you've got to learn to share."

His lips claimed hers again and from somewhere far away, she heard Lori clapping her hands. "All right, people, nothing to see here! Show's over, give the birds some privacy—the lovebirds, I mean, not the penguins."

Gracie smiled around Carter's kiss, happiness bringing her lips back to his. Her fingers curled into the collar of his shirt and she breathed in the warm, fresh scent of his aftershave, a prayer of thankfulness welling in her heart. They still had some issues to work through, but for the first time in all her years of knowing Carter, Gracie felt confident enough to leave the past behind and embrace the future—whatever it might hold.

Carter turned slightly, breaking the contact but tightening his grip around her waist. His forehead rested against hers and he closed his eyes. "I always hoped we'd find our way here someday."

"Our way back, you mean. We've been here before, we just fought the truth." She rubbed her nose against his teasingly. "Some of us more than others."

He growled low in the back of his throat. "Hey now, watch it. How about a compromise?"

"I'm wearing a rock on my left finger. So sure, whatever you say." Gracie grinned, loving that his embrace around her had yet to loosen.

Carter nuzzled her cheek, his stubble rough but endearing against her skin. "We'll call it a return."

Gracie stared up into his eyes, hoping the emotion clogging her heart made it to her eyes. "A return. I like that."

"To friendship."

She closed her eyes and burrowed further into his embrace. "And to love."

* * * * *

Dear Reader,

I had a blast researching the penguins at the Aquarium of the Americas for this novel! Penguins have always been one of my favorite animals and are a huge collectible around my house. Thanks again to penguin keeper Tom Dyer for allowing me to use the current names of the penguins at the aquarium. Be sure to stop by next time you're in New Orleans and meet the real Huey and the rest of the gang. (Gumbo is the only fictional penguin name used in this book.)

This story was exciting for me to write because New Orleans will always hold a special place in my heart. It's where a lot of my husband's family live, and it's where he proposed, right there aboard the steamboat Natchez. We took a dinner cruise and, after a stroll around the deck, he dropped down on one knee and popped the question. What memories!

I hope that after reading this story you'll have experienced a taste of the delightful Cajun atmosphere of New Orleans, and understand why Gracie, Carter and I love it so much.

Blessings!

Betsy St. Amant

QUESTIONS FOR DISCUSSION

1. Carter left his hometown because of his father's secret lifestyle. What could he have done instead to work through the issue and avoid leaving his family and friends behind?

2. Gracie developed issues with forgiveness after feeling abandoned by Carter in high school. How did she carry those issues along with her into her adult life? What should she have done to work through them?

3. Carter gave up his career of riches and fame after he got his life straightened out. What things do new Christians often sacrifice in order to follow God?

4. Gracie harbored secret feelings for Carter for years that went beyond friendship. Has there ever been a time in your life when you had to risk embarrassment to tell someone you cared for them? How did that person receive the news?

5. Carter and Gracie shared a close friendship as children/teenagers before realizing it had developed into something more. Do you believe men and women can share a close friendship and not have it turn into romantic feelings?

6. Carter felt betrayed by his father because of his father's secret gambling addiction. Have you ever felt betrayed or offended by a pastor or family member? If so, how did you handle the negative emotions?

7. Do you believe pastors and church leaders are called to a

higher level of morals because of their leadership positions?

8. Gracie grew close to Reverend Alexander because she grew up without a father. Has anyone ever stepped in to fill various father- or mother-figure roles in your life? How do you feel about those people now?

9. Have you ever struggled with forgiving someone? If so, how did you handle it?

10. In the story, Gracie and Carter confided in their best friends along the way. Who in your life provides your moral support?

11. Why was it so hard for Gracie to believe the negative truth about Carter's father?

12. Carter made mistakes in his past that he will always regret. What is one mistake in your life that you will never forget? How can you use that memory in a positive way?

13. Gracie loved the city of New Orleans. Have you ever visited New Orleans? What is your favorite city to visit? What cultural influences make that city unique?

14. Gracie was a penguin keeper at the Aquarium of the Americas—her dream job. What would your career be if you could have your choice?

15. Gracie's insecurity led her to feel threatened by Tawny, a woman who was much more confident in herself. Have you ever felt intimidated by another person you felt was

more attractive than you? How is that kind of comparison dangerous to your emotional well-being? To your spiritual life?

Dumped via certified letter days before her wedding, Haley Scott sees her dreams of happily ever after crushed. But could it turn out to be the best thing that's ever happened to her?

Turn the page for a sneak preview of
AN UNEXPECTED MATCH
by Dana Corbit,
book 1 in the new
WEDDING BELLS BLESSINGS *trilogy,*
available beginning August 2009
from Love Inspired®

"Is there a Haley Scott here?"

Haley glanced through the storm door at the package carrier before opening the latch and letting in some of the frigid March wind.

"That's me, but not for long."

The blank stare the man gave her as he stood on the porch of her mother's new house only made Haley smile. In fifty-one hours and twenty-nine minutes, her name would be changing. Her life as well, but she couldn't allow herself to think about that now.

She wouldn't attribute her sudden shiver to anything but the cold, either. Not with a bridal fitting to endure, embossed napkins to pick up and a caterer to call. Too many details, too little time and certainly no time for her to entertain her silly cold feet.

"Then this is for you."

Practiced at this procedure after two days back in her Markston, Indiana, hometown, Haley reached out both arms to accept a bridal gift, but the carrier turned and deposited an overnight letter package in just one of her hands. Haley stared down at the Michigan return address of her fiancé, Tom Jeffries.

"Strange way to send a wedding present," she murmured.

The man grunted and shoved an electronic signature device at her, waiting until she scrawled her name.

As soon as she closed the door, Haley returned to the living room and yanked the tab on the paperboard. From it, she withdrew a single sheet of folded notebook paper.

Something inside her suggested that she should sit down to read it, so she lowered herself into a floral side chair. Hesitating, she glanced at the far wall where wedding gifts in pastel-colored paper were stacked, then she unfolded the note. Her stomach tightened as she read each handwritten word.

"*Best?* He signed it *best?*" Her voice cracked as the paper fluttered to the floor. She was sure she should be sobbing or collapsing in a heap, but she felt only numb as she stared down at the offending piece of paper.

The letter that had changed everything.

"Best what?" Trina Scott asked as she padded into the room with fuzzy striped socks on her feet. "Sweetie?"

Haley lifted her gaze to meet her mother's and could see concern etched between her carefully tweezed brows.

"What's the matter?" Trina shot a glance toward the foyer, her chin-length brown hair swinging past her ear as she did it. "Did I just hear someone at the door?"

Haley tilted her head to indicate the sheet of paper on the floor. "It's from Tom. He called off the wedding."

"What? Why?" Trina began, but then brushed her hand through the air twice as if to erase the question. "That's not the most important thing right now, is it?"

Haley stared at her mother. A little pity wouldn't have been out of place here. Instead of offering any, Trina snapped up the letter and began to read. When she finished, she sat on the cream-colored sofa opposite Haley's chair.

"I don't approve of his methods." She shook the letter to emphasize her point. "And I always thought the boy didn't have enough good sense to come out of the rain, but I have to agree with him on this one. You two aren't right for each other."

Haley couldn't believe her ears. Okay, Tom wouldn't have been the partner Trina Scott would have chosen for her youngest daughter if Trina's grand matchmaking scheme hadn't gone belly-up. Still, Haley hadn't realized how strongly her mother disapproved of her choice.

"No sense being upset about my opinion now," Trina told her. "I kept praying that you'd make the right decision, but I guess Tom made it for you. Now we have to get busy. There are a lot of calls to make. I'll call Amy." Trina dug the cell phone from her purse and hit one of the speed dial numbers.

Haley winced. In any situation, it shouldn't have surprised her that her mother's first reaction was to phone her best friend, but Trina had more than knee-jerk reasons to make this call. Not only had Amy Warren been asked to join them downtown this afternoon for Haley's final bridal fitting, but she also was scheduled to make the wedding cake at her bakery, Amy's Elite Treats.

Haley asked herself again why she'd agreed to plan the wedding in her hometown. Now her humiliation would double as she shared it with family friends. One in particular.

"May I speak to Amy?" Trina began as someone answered the line. "Oh, Matthew, is that you?"

That's the one. Haley squeezed her eyes shut.

* * * * *

*Will her former crush be the one
to mend Haley's broken heart?
Find out in AN UNEXPECTED MATCH,
available in August 2009
only from Love Inspired®.*